Strangers
in
Paradise

Also by Lauren O. Thyme

The Lemurian Way: Remembering your Essential Nature
Along the Nile
Cosmic Grandma Wisdom
Twin Souls: A Karmic Love Story
Forgiveness Equals Fortune, co-authored with Liah Holtzman
Thymely Tales: Transformational Fairy Tales for Adults and Children
From the Depths of Thyme: Poems of Life, Sex, and Transformation
Alternatives for Everyone
Coming soon: *Catherine, a true story*

Strangers
in
Paradise

Lauren O. Thyme

Lauren O. Thyme Publishing
Santa Fe
2017

Strangers in Paradise © 2017 Lauren O. Thyme

ISBN 978-0-9983446-0-7

Interior and Cover Design by Sue Stein
Cover photo by Lauren O. Thyme

Lauren O. Thyme Publishing
Santa Fe, New Mexico
www.laurenothymecreations.com
thyme.lauren@gmail.com
Facebook Lauren O. Thyme

Contents

Prologue

Mahina's Story

I remember my beloved clearly, as though he is standing in front of me. His black hair was long, cut back from his face, hanging straight down his back. He was much taller than me; the top of my small head came only to his massive shoulders. He would often pick me up to kiss me. "My little bird," he called me. I loved to touch his arms and smooth, hairless chest; he would flex his muscles to make them jump. His dancing eyes were dark like mine, open and trusting. I could sometimes see myself mirrored in them, like the clear pond near the waterfall. He had a cleft in his chin, as if the gods had an afterthought when they finished sculpting his face. He was, without a doubt, the most handsome man in our village.

We had grown up with each other, inseparable friends since we were small children. We had played together in the sand, picked papayas, and swam in the warm, blue ocean.

As we grew older, our play became more intimate. I was still a young wahini when we began our touching games. Often we would swim out beyond the breakers, and turn over, floating on our backs. The brilliant sky above us was thick with clouds, which would form and reform into fantastic shapes as we watched. Then he would dive underneath me, pretending to be a shark. He would nip at my firm behind and swelling hips, or run his hands over my developing breasts, making gooseflesh rise on my skin. Or he would tickle me around my ribs, making me laugh and sputter, as I swallowed sea water. Then we would race back through the waves to the sand, where we would chase one other around the palm trees, biting and tickling, fighting and punching each other in mock battle, as those in love know how to do.

I was yet older when we coupled for the first time. On the cliff, in the wide sacred circle of black stones where the grass grew thick and green, we laid down and gave ourselves to each other. Joy and satisfaction intermingled. His young manhood erupted after only a moment the first time he entered me, but we would learn how to extend our pleasure. I didn't know what felt better, my enjoyment, or giving pleasure to him. We took turns learning how to delight each other with our hands, tongues, and bodies, during the long, gentle tropical nights, concealed from the village cooking fires and prying eyes. I thought I could never be happier.

And yet I was to learn that I could be much happier.

Our families decided that we should mate. His family and mine had been friends for many generations, but he and I would be the first to blend the blood lines. My mother sent my sisters out to comb the island for white orchids to make my wedding lei. She and my female relatives spent days preparing the food for the feast. The wild pigs had cooked all day in their underground oven. Hungry guests could find the special event by their noses, but they would have to wait until the ceremony was complete.

The sky was swirled with pink and lavender as the day was coming to an end. My love and I stood together, hand in hand, glowing in that pink shimmer of light. The village people gathered around us on the beach. I could hear the lap, lap of the waves, gently patting the shore. The Kahuna said his special words that joined the two of us together forever, wrapping a long tapa cloth around us and tying it in a knot. Our families cheered and kissed us. Then the dancing and feasting began.

Joy is a hard word to define. If you've never experienced it, then I cannot tell you how joyful I felt. If you have felt joy, then I tell you that I felt joy, and more than joy. I felt the bliss of complete union of souls. The knowledge that our hearts would now beat as one made me happy, as a bird that flies without tiring. Like the wise and playful smiling fish who leaps from the ocean.

I don't remember anyone else that evening, although I know the whole village was there, including our family and friends, noisily talking, laughing, and eating. I only remember him. My husband. My one great, true love. A soul had been divided into halves and had taken up residence in two homes, my own feminine body and his solid, masculine one. We had become one entity. When he was happy, I was happy. When we joined our bodies in love, I felt the complete merging of our joint soul, as the separation of our skins dissolved in the ecstasy of love-making.

I recall how we lay together all that night in our new hut, listening to the sounds of the drums. We didn't sleep but touched and caressed each other with newfound exhilaration. Tickling and laughing like the children that we still were. Time became motionless.

Before my wedding, my mother had advised me to always bring happiness to my husband, as though this would be a difficult task. Bringing delight to my beloved only brought great joy to me. For effortless days and nights we cuddled, and talked, and made love again and again. When we made love, we talked often of the children we would have. Children to further our blood line. Children to share our love with.

When we parted for even a moment, I felt pain. The pain of as-yet unsatisfied hunger. The cessation of bliss. The awareness of our temporary separation. Our private world was our hut and the sea. Fortunately, during that first week, our friends and loved ones left us food outside the flap of our new home, so we never had to fend for ourselves, never had to leave each other.

The temperature was getting hotter. The ocean, only a few feet away, was meant for us to swim in together. To refresh our bodies in the glistening water. One day the sun shone so brightly that my husband felt compelled to swim, to cool the intense heat from his brown body. But I was lazy and told him to swim without me and I soon fell asleep.

My nap was disturbed by wailing outside my hut. I woke up and went to the entryway. The sun was low in the sky. I had slept all afternoon.

I peered out of the flap. Some of the men from the village were gathered in the water. Making a great commotion. Thrashing around. Calling anxiously to one another. I slipped on my sarong and went out. When I appeared, I saw women weeping. When they saw me, they turned their faces away. In the crowd, I could see my father, who was taller than most of the men.

He stepped out of the sea and came up to me, still dripping with salt water. He grasped me firmly by my shoulders as though sensing I might run away. "My daughter." He stopped and gulped twice. His eyes were moist with feeling.

I turned my head to the side, refusing to look at his eyes, cold chills running over my skin, terrible premonitions engulfing me.

"Mano, the shark..."

"I don't want to listen! Let me go!" I cried.

He continued relentlessly. "Mano has taken your husband to live with him in the deep," he said simply, but his face was contorted with emotion.

"No, you lie..." I started to cry out, but I knew what he said was true, and stopped resisting, my body turning to dark stone, like those at the sacred circles.

"Little One, I am so sorry." My father let go of me, and his arms sagged to his side. Suddenly he looked old, his wrinkles well-worn paths woven deep into his face.

The warm air had become chilled and I shivered. I put my arms around myself to get warm. My body was as heavy as the sacred stones and my mind was blank, as though I didn't know myself anymore. Everyone seemed far away, like the holy mountain behind me, shrouded in misty clouds. I held my mouth so tightly that my jaws hurt.

I looked out at the ocean. The waves were coming in, one after another the way they always had, always would. But now the sea was my enemy. It didn't care it had stolen him from me. I was torn from my essence. Adrift in a suddenly alien world. Alone...

Chapter 1

Dr. Eberhardt's Diagnosis

The first thing Sarah Arlington experienced when she walked down the steps of the turbo-prop into Lihue airport was the gentle evening air. The soothing breeze caressed her skin gently like a seasoned lover, playfully swirling her long red hair around her face.

Sarah closed her eyes for a moment, reveling in the sensuous feeling of the warm tropical night. Kauai felt like a comfortable friend, something she'd never experienced in bustling, smoggy Los Angeles or, for that matter, anywhere else she'd traveled. She could smell the scent of flowers blooming in the dark around the edges of the small, open terminal and heard crickets chirping in nearby bushes. She bought a sweet-smelling plumeria lei from one of the vendors and hung it around her neck, holding it up with both hands, deeply inhaling their heavily perfumed fragrance. "I'm home," she sighed.

With a sudden rasp of mechanisms rusty from the salt air, the baggage carousel starting moving as luggage was disgorged from the parked aircraft. The former journalist collected her two bags and looked around for the Avis counter.

She wearily rubbed her bloodshot eyes as the agent finalized her paperwork. "Kauai sure looks different from the last time I was here," Sarah commented.

"When was that?" asked the impassive Asian rental agent behind the counter.

"A day or so after Hurricane Iniki had hit."

"No kidding! You were here then?" He stopped writing and shook his head, his slanted eyes wide in amazement.

"I came here on assignment. To report the disaster for my newspaper."

"From the mainland?"

"Uh, huh. California."

"Yeah, I read all about it," he continued. "I was still living in Honolulu. Hadn't moved here yet. What a mess."

"It sure was," Sarah agreed, remembering the devastation.

"You'll find it quite different now."

"I certainly hope so," and the two of them chuckled.

She heaved her luggage into the trunk of the rental car and started the engine, adjusted the mirrors, and fastened her seat belt. Sarah gently brought the lei up to her nose again, enjoying the intoxicating aroma. "Nothing on earth smells like this." The sun had already set so she couldn't see the ocean, but she got a whiff of the sweet clean air from the open window.

Her flight from Los Angeles to Honolulu had seemed to take forever, and then she had to take the smaller prop-jet for Kauai. Fatigue reddened her eyes. Fortunately she only had a short ride to the Poipu Sheraton.

"Will you be staying with us long, Miss Arlington?" asked the elegant young Asian woman at the front desk.

"I'm not sure." She signed the registration card, noticing a huge vase of flowers next to her on the highly polished desk. "What a lovely bouquet," she exclaimed. "What are these?" She pointed to elongated, red flame-shaped flowers in the arrangement.

"Those are ginger."

"Are they fragrant?" She tried to smell them, but the stems were too tall.

"No. They're known primarily for their beauty. They last a long time, too. We have a florist shop here, if you'd like to order some for your room." The clerk smiled and handed Sarah her key. "Enjoy your stay," and she motioned to a burly Polynesian bellhop who picked up the two heavy bags with ease.

"Thank you very much. I hope to." After Sarah had closed and locked her door, she wearily peeled off her clothes and stepped into the shower. The hot water streamed onto her aching head and shoulders, relaxing her. Then she stretched her shoulders back, hearing the vertebrae pop back into place. After she had dried off, she stretched her long, graceful body onto the comfortable king-size bed, grateful at its massive comfort, and turned out the light, exhausted, and ready for sleep.

A rainstorm had begun while she was in the shower. Sarah could hear rain pouring heavily through the palm trees outside, tapping on the hotel windows. Except for the sound of falling rain, the room was still. The fragrance of the lei permeated the darkened room.

Lying on her back, with her arm flung across her blue-green eyes, Sarah listened to the hypnotic rhythm of the rain. Although she was exhausted and ready for sleep, her mind refused to succumb; the tumultuous events of the last week forced their way into her consciousness. Especially the conversation with Dr. Eberhardt, the conversation that had irrevocably altered her life.

"Okay, I've submitted to all your horrible tests. So tell me. Why am

I having these headaches?" she had asked the physician bluntly, facing him across the massive oak desk in his office.

The doctor cleared his throat, closed her file in front of him, and removed his reading glasses. "I'm really sorry, Miss Arlington. I'm afraid I have bad news." He paused. "You have cancer. The tumor is growing in your brain, here." He pointed to the front of his own head. "It's rather large and growing fast. Unfortunately it's inoperable due to its location." He nervously played with a paper clip on his desk. He hated these difficult encounters and wished he was on the golf course or anywhere else but here. He examined Sarah's face. *Too bad,* he thought. *She's a beautiful woman.*

Sarah Arlington swallowed hard, but her reporter's no-nonsense approach to catastrophes wouldn't fail her, even at this moment. "Okay. What's the bottom line? Am I'm going to die?"

"We can never know for sure. You have a 30% chance of survival. This kind of cancer doesn't respond too well to chemotherapy, but radiation has greater efficacy."

"Will that work? Get rid of the cancer, I mean."

"We can't guarantee that." He pulled the paper clip apart. "But as a palliative therapy, I recommend it."

"What does that mean?" Sarah found herself annoyed at his medical double-talk.

"We will try to shrink the tumor somewhat, to reduce your pain and prevent other symptoms. If the radiation doesn't cure it, at least it will make you more comfortable."

"But will that ensure I'll live?"

He shrugged. "We don't know. Each case is always different."

The redheaded woman felt insulted at being referred to as a case, and drummed her fingers on his desk. "So, how long could I live if I don't have radiation?"

"Mmmm. It's hard to say. Maybe three to six months. Maybe a little longer. The mass is close to the optic nerve, so your eyesight will probably go first. Double vision. Loss of peripheral vision. That sort of thing. Towards the end you'll probably lose your sight altogether."

"Blind," she grimaced. Her eyes started to well up in spite of herself. She pushed away wispy tendrils of hair the color of bright new pennies, and quickly wiped away the renegade tears, which leaked down her slender cheeks.

"I recommend you start treatment immediately. You shouldn't wait. The symptoms will only get worse." He glanced at his watch.

Sarah's jaw muscles tensed and her eyes got a hard look to them. "So I better not waste any more time."

That's what Eric had said when she had refused his engagement ring. His words echoed in her memory.

"We're just wasting time. Why not marry me now?" Eric had asked a little harshly. "I've been waiting for you long enough already. You're being stubborn, as usual," he argued.

"I'm just not ready," had been Sarah's reply. "Besides, my career is finally taking off. Let's not quarrel about this again."

"I'm not quarreling," he began.

"Sounds like it to me," she interrupted.

"You're afraid of making a commitment," he retorted acidly.

"That's not true," she protested.

He gave up, realizing that she wasn't going to relent. "Sarah, you're not getting any younger, you know. Better not wait too long," he had said with a sharp edge to his voice. When she didn't reply, he abruptly got up and left her sitting alone in the restaurant.

That was the last time she had seen Eric. Except a year later, when she had accidentally run into him at O'Briens Bar. He was with a blonde. Sarah could see the sparkle of diamonds on the young woman's third right finger and the adoring way she looked at Eric. "Well, he sure didn't waste any time," she thought sarcastically

"Miss Arlington?" The doctor was trying to get her attention.

"What?" Startled out of her reverie, Sarah looked up. "Oh, sorry, doctor. What were you saying?"

"I said, my nurse will schedule you for your radiation treatments. We'll try to shrink that mass, which should help relieve your headaches."

She remembered interviewing cancer patients, and the horror stories they told her of cancer treatments. Many of them had died anyway even with therapy. "Will those treatments make me lose my hair or throw up?"

"Yes, probably. Whether you start experiencing nausea or vomiting will depend on the progress of the tumor."

Sarah scrunched up her mouth, the way she always did when she was annoyed. "No, I can't do it." The tall woman stood up decisively, towering over the seated physician.

"But, without treatment you're..."

"I can't do it!" Sarah bolted before Dr. Eberhardt could stop her. She ran out of his office, past the waiting patients, headed for the front door. The doctor was right behind her. Tears of anger were stinging her cheeks as she reached for the down button of the elevator when he caught up to her.

"Please, Sarah," he said. "You mustn't let this go. It could be dangerous. You should have radiation therapy."

"I won't do it," she cried. "You can't make me!" She sounded hysterical, even to herself.

Dr. Eberhardt gripped her arm, but she shrugged it off.

The elevator had arrived. The last thing Sarah saw was the doctor's pained expression as the doors closed, blocking him out.

Somehow she found her car in the parking garage and drove savagely away. Her nostrils flared; the fear temporarily pushed away, replaced by rage.

"You don't have much time to waste." In her mind's eye, she melodramatically visualized an hourglass with the sand running out.

A flashflood of emotions enveloped her and she made an impulsive decision. She drove to the newspaper office and collected her few possessions in a box. Then she marched into Sam Johnston's office, her senior editor. "I quit," she announced loudly, dropping the box on his desk with a loud thump.

"What? Sit down, Sarah. You look like a herd of elephants ready to stampede." His aging face and sagging jowls always reminded her of a bloodhound.

"I'm going to Hawaii," she replied tersely, continuing to stand.

Sam stared at her reddened eyes. "Have you been crying? What's wrong, honey?"

She ignored his questions. "Kauai actually. I've always wanted to go back. Ever since I covered the hurricane." She was talking very fast.

"Whoa, you're not making any sense. What's the hurry?" He stood up and came around his desk.

"I've waited too long and I don't have any time——to waste, and anyway, the doctor said my hair will fall out." She grabbed a handful of her luxuriant red mane to make her point.

The editor finally understood the gist of her wild babbling. "The headaches? Oh, Sarah, I'm sorry." He reached around her shoulder in a sympathetic gesture, but she jerked away, afraid she would break down in tears for sure.

"I don't want you to feel sorry for me. I have to make the best of…it. And I want to go back. I've been obsessed with Kauai ever since I returned."

"Sure, sure," replied Sam, in a soothing voice. "Take a few weeks off, you'll be good as new. Then you can come back and…"

"Don't patronize me!" Then the tears started again, and she furiously wiped them away. "There's nothing to come back to."

"Shouldn't you think about this?" He sat on the corner of his desk. "That's a pretty big decision."

"No. I've spent too much time thinking and not enough time living."

"Is there anyone you can call?"

"My mother, but we haven't talked in years. She's too busy with her new husband." Sarah shrugged. "And you know how much I've been working and traveling. Not much time for friends, either." Her voice was shrill with emotion.

"Sure, I know, honey." He changed the subject, uncertain how to proceed. He decided on a more practical avenue. "Okay. You have a paycheck coming tomorrow. Plus severance pay too, you know. And you're eligible for health insurance which will cover you for the next eighteen months." He ticked off the points on his fingers.

"If I live that long," she said grimly.

He gasped at her curt reply. "Sarah! I'm just trying to help."

"Forgive me, Sam. You're absolutely right. I'm acting like my problem is all your fault." She hugged him. "Thanks for everything. You're a great guy."

"So when you get settled, call me with your address and phone number. I want to stay in touch with you."

"I will, Sam. You're sweet."

He was about to say something more, but she interrupted him. "I'll be okay, Sam. You know me. I'm strong." Even though Sarah was several decades younger than the senior editor, she maternally patted his rugged face and forced herself to smile.

"Is there anything? Anything at all that I can do?"

"No thanks, Sam. There's nothing much to do I guess."

"Best of luck, Sarah."

"Thanks, Sam. I'll need it." Then she hefted the box and disappeared through the doorway.

The next ten days were frenetic. Sorting through her possessions. Selling some furniture, giving some away, and having Salvation Army retrieve the rest. Even selling her car, although she'd gritted her teeth at the price she had finally settled for. When she was done, she had bought a one-way ticket to Kauai.

Which brings me up to this minute. She yawned, her jaw crackling. *Have I made a mistake?"*she asked herself. *I don't know.* The downpour had abated, and crickets were singing their love songs again. Sarah fell asleep in the big bed in Poipu, her luxuriant red hair spread out across the white pillows like a volcanic eruption.

Chapter 2

Kamalani Waikoloa

Sarah slept deeply in her hotel room, not even waking when the brilliant morning light beamed through a crack in the curtains. She was dreaming of watching an old newsreel of Hitler's storm troopers invading Poland. Soldiers marched in perfect goose-stepping precision through the occupied streets. Tanks fired and buildings collapsed. Then, as dreams do, the scene changed. Nazis began parachuting into Lihue airport, finding their way to her hotel. In the dream, soldiers brok into her hotel room and pointed their automatic rifles at her head, when she forced herself to wake up, sweating. Her hair clung to her forehead and neck.

After the dream, Sarah couldn't go back to sleep. She tried unsuccessfully, tossing and turning for a while, then got up, and took a shower. Afterwards she put on a simple, white linen dress and sandals, and went out to the rented car.

The rain had stopped hours earlier and the sky was the color of spring irises. A golden sheen glittered on luxuriant green foliage. Birds flitted through the trees, calling melodiously to one another.

"Who could think of anything bad on a day like today?" She smiled in spite of herself, and felt a contentment she hadn't experienced since she was a young child. In the distance she could see a stately mountain, the peak covered over with whipped marshmallow clouds. "Where should I go?" she asked herself. The map from the car rental agency lay next to her. "I'll just drive until I find something interesting."

She drove to Highway 50, through the famous tunnel of trees, the tops of the foliage touching overhead. When she saw a sign that said, "Opeakaa Falls, 2 miles," she turned and followed the road. When she got to the scenic turnout, she parked the car and went over to the protective rail.

Several hundred yards below her, the lush Wailua valley extended out to the ocean. A green checkerboard of grass, taro fields, rice and sugar cane were gently blowing in the restless wind. Wandering lazily through the valley was the Wailua river with a few canoers paddling along its tranquil waters.

From a distance she could hear Opeakaa Falls, towering over the entire valley. Three separate waterways coursed over enormous boulders before crashing down into the valley. Sarah felt the power of water cascading over the cliffs and breathed deeply. A deepening sense of aliveness coursed through her. She could practically see her veins pound in unison with the vigor of the waterfall. She focused her Nikon, and took a number of pictures of the waterfall, the camera capturing the sparkling grandeur on film.

A couple of elderly tourists nodded as they walked past her, got into their car, and left, bringing her awareness back to her situation. *What am I doing?* she thought. *I must be crazy, running away, dumping everything I worked so hard for.* She sighed. *Still, this island is so beautiful. I could live here forever.* She hesitated. *Or until, whenever.* She pulled her shoulders straight. *Something will work out. It always does.*

She waved to the couple as their car pulled onto the highway, then noticed a large cluster of palm trees in a clearing near the road. Sunlight drifted through the tree. Here and there were puddles of shadow. Beyond the trees was a circle of huge lava rocks, piled on top of one another, creating an enclosure. Parts of the surround had collapsed and Sarah judged that the circle must be quite old.

A mist, created from the recent rain and warmth, drifted between the trees, partially hiding the area, generating an other-worldly atmosphere. The light dimmed as the sun slid behind clouds. Sarah was inexplicably drawn to the stones and starting walking towards them.

Suddenly, out of the mist, as if a magician had waved a wand, a tall Hawaiian man materialized. She gasped, and stopped, staring rudely at the apparition. Her hand reached out involuntarily to touch him, to see if he was real.

Birds-of-paradise bloomed riotously on his unbuttoned shirt. As a breeze caught the fabric, she could see his brown chest was completely hairless and smooth, the pectoral muscles well-developed. Broad shoulders strained against the cloth, trying to break free. Wrinkled khaki shorts fit tightly over his muscular thighs. His typically Polynesian face looked youthful, ageless. His thick, black hair ruffled in the breeze. Slightly slanted, dark eyes roamed over her body. As he unself-consciously examined Sarah's shapely bare legs beneath her short dress, she felt a mild throbbing.

"Hi," the apparition spoke, breaking the spell. He grinned with self-assurance, dimples etched into the finely chiseled face, white teeth gleaming against fleshy lips.

"Hello," she replied softly, hardly recognizing her voice. Behind her was the commanding sound of the waterfall. She caught a faint whiff of plumerias and she remembered the lei she had left back in the hotel room. She licked her lips and cleared her throat, trying to think of something to say. But all she could focus on was a tingling sensation in her hands, as she ached to touch the glossy skin of his muscular chest.

"You know, for a moment I thought you were Pele," he said, in a teasing tone.

"Who?" She shook her head, not understanding his meaning.

"Pele, the Hawaiian goddess of volcanoes and fire. She has red hair like you." He chuckled. "I thought you were, I mean, you look like Pele, coming to visit the sacred place here." He indicated the stone circle behind him.

Sarah smiled, her high cheekbones standing in relief as she did so. Her blue-green eyes sparkled. "Well, a lot of people have accused me of being hotheaded."

"Really…" he replied slowly. "You seem perfect to me."

"You must think I'm pretty weird, though, standing here staring at you, with my mouth hanging open." She awkwardly shifted her weight back and forth, first on one foot, then the other, while still holding the camera in her left hand.

"That makes two weird people, then." He threw his head back and laughed out loud for the simple joy of it. His voice was deeply melodious and his laughter infectious.

Sarah couldn't help but laugh with him. She held out her right hand, still smiling. "Sarah Arlington. Reporter. I mean, former reporter. And tourist."

"Kamalani Waikoloa. Guardian of this glorious island." The Polynesian man took her hand with both of his large, brown ones. He slowly examined her long, slender fingers, the slim wrist, the creamy, pale skin of her arm, running his free hand over her fingers. "My friends call me Lani." He looked into her eyes, without giving back her hand. "You know, your eyes are the color of the ocean inside the reefs over there."

"Uh, huh," she replied, trying to overlook the sensations sprinting down her arms and through her loins. She pursed her lips. She felt aroused as she stood there, while the audacious stranger held her hand. "Could I have my hand back?"

Lani didn't let go but pretended to examine her fingers. "Hey lady? You need manicure? Know da kine one. She do good job," he said, pretending to talk pidgin.

Sarah couldn't help giggling. "Sorry, won't work," and retrieved her electrified hand.

"Well, Little Lady, ya can't blame a feller fer tryin," he replied, trying to sound like John Wayne. He stuffed his hands in his hip pockets, pretending he had six-shooters in them. His mahogany-colored eyes danced with mischief.

They both laughed again.

"Sarah Arlington." He teased outrageously with her, batting his eyes like a southern belle. "Lawdy, Miss Scarlet! Your name sounds like you should be dressed in hoop skirts, drinking mint juleps on the veranda of some Southern plantation."

She simply smiled in reply, but his flirtatious manner and humorous impressions made her heart flutter.

Then Lani searched so deeply into her aquamarine eyes with his own liquid brown ones that Sarah started to feel uncomfortable. "I have a hunch I know you. Do you live on the big island?"

"No."

"Did we go to college together?"

"I went to school in California."

"Maybe we attended a symposium last year."

"I wasn't in the islands last year."

He frowned. "I'm convinced we've met before, someplace. You seem incredibly familiar."

"I'm pretty sure I don't know you."

"Are you positive?"

"Well, almost," she replied. "I've only been to Kauai once years ago, and I don't think I met you then. Although, you look familiar to me, too. Strange, isn't it?"

"Very."

"I never forget a face, but I don't have a place or date to connect you with. I'm stumped." She furrowed her eyebrows.

He reached over to smooth out the furrow. "That's better. You're much too pretty to have your face creased like that."

A sweet warmth from his hand spread down her face. She searched his eyes for clues to explain why his touch was so pleasing.

He smiled, his eyes dancing under her scrutiny, crinkling at the corners, dimples carved deep into his face.

An irresistible urge to touch those dimples overtook her. Sarah felt as though she was mesmerized. His playful manner encouraged her, and she tentatively explored the tiny facial caverns with her fingertip.

He closed his eyes, allowing the intimacy, until she was satisfied. With a jerk, she remembered herself. "I'm sorry," she apologized lamely, quickly pulling her hand back. "I don't usually touch strangers."

He opened his slightly slanted lids and gazed thoughtfully at her. "It's okay. Felt good." Lani changed the subject. "So, Sarah Arlington, former reporter and tourist. Even though we're not well acquainted, would you allow me to show you around my island?"

"I don't know," Sarah began. The breeze blew his shirt open, exposing his smooth skin. The urge to touch him grew overwhelming again. She tried to ignore the outlines of taut muscles around his chest and abdomen.

"Just say yes."

Later when she would think about this moment, her decision would seem completely irrational. But tremors of excitement quaked through her body, leaving no doubt as to what her answer would be. "Yes," she whispered.

"Excellent choice," he said exhaling. He pulled her arm through his and turned them around, guiding them to the circle of stones.

Sarah felt oddly comfortable with her arm linked in his, as though they were old friends meeting again after a long absence. She examined his face in profile. He had a regally sculpted jaw, cleanly shaven, with a dark stain of beard beneath the skin, straight nose, and wide, sensuous lips surrounded by the delightful dimples.

He interrupted her scrutiny with a lecture. "This is called a heiau," he said, sweeping his free hand to indicate the stone circle. "The Poliahu heiau. It's a sacred place, created by Kahunas many centuries ago." He sounded like he'd practiced his speech before.

"Who are Kahunas?"

"They're priests, wise men, in charge of the island's spiritual life. The word Kahuna means keeper of the secrets."

"Sort of like a shaman or medicine man?"

"Exactly."

"When did they live?"

"Oh, some are still alive and well, continuing to perform their mystical practices. My grandfather's a Kahuna, and so was my great-grandfather."

She raised her eyebrows. "I thought they were all in the past."

"Oh, no, although they almost died out after the haoles came. White men. But they're still quite powerful in the islands. And they continue our spiritual customs passed down through many generations."

As they got closer to the sacred circle of stones, the sun broke through a cloud, flooding the area in bright sunshine. Small insects buzzed around them.

"I'm getting goose bumps all over," Sarah mentioned.

"This particular heiau is a special one. Its power was intentionally created by ceremonies and prayers." He lowered his voice. "Grandfather has never said so, but I think there were blood sacrifices done here, too."

"Oooo." She shivered, and stopped walking, like a balky horse.

"I don't mean nowadays." He laughed. "Come on, silly," and towed her along. "This particular heiau served te Alii Nui."

"Who are a-le-e newee?" She tried to imitate the word.

"The royalty. Kings and queens of Kauai. See that area over there?" She looked to see where he was pointing.

"That's the royal birthing place. Queens would come here to give birth to their babies, surrounded by midwives and Kahunas."

"So, what are you doing here?"

"My grandfather asked me to bring some flowers. Here they are." He pointed to rocks piled up in a particular design, with flowers carefully arranged on them.

She noticed more flowers, and food, too, placed on other rock formations. "Who brought these?"

"Locals. It's like lighting candles in a Catholic church. Brings much mana."

"What's mana?"

"Good fortune."

"Hmmm. Maybe I should bring flowers, too. I could use some mana." She rubbed her chilled arms. "I don't know if it's my imagination, but..." she hesitated

"What?"

"I want to walk sideways around the heiau."

"Yes, that's how ordinary people have to approach the heiau, to show respect."

"And I can almost hear a humming, or singing in my ears. Does that sound crazy?"

He smiled knowingly. "You must be intuitive, tuning in to the ancient stones. Humming and chanting was part of all the sacred ceremonies, done by both the Kahunas and the islanders. However, only Alii Nui and Kahunas could go inside this stone enclosure."

She looked inside. "When was the last birthing ceremony?"

"I don't know. But Hawaiian royalty was dispensed with in the late 1800s."

She tried to visualize what the heiau must have looked like in its prime, her back to him.

Lani examined her surreptitiously. She was tall and slender with a narrow waist and shapely hips. "Come on, I'll take you to Waimea canyon. Walk like this." He began to walk backwards, without turning his back on the heiau.

She followed suit, without question.

Once they had gotten to the edge of the trees, he turned around and walked normally. "Why don't you leave your car here. We can come back later and pick it up."

"All right." Captivated, Sarah might agree to anything the young islander suggested. Later when she was alone in her hotel room she would muse, *I went with him without even knowing him or anything about him.*

Lani walked over to a black four-wheel drive SUV, splattered red with mud from the recent rain, and opened the door for her. "Your carriage awaits, Madame," and he bowed playfully.

"Thank you, sir," she replied in kind, smiling, and got in.

"First I'm going to take you to see Waimea Canyon. It's Kauai's most famous landmark."

He drove past fields of sugar cane, the mature tips flowing in the wind.

"What is that big mountain that has clouds all over it?" Sarah asked.

"That's Mount Waialeale, our holy mountain."

"Why-a-lee-a-lee," she repeated.

"Very good," he praised her. "You talk like a native already."

Sarah grinned.

"There's another heiau at the top of the mountain, but it's hard to climb up to. Mt. Waialeale is the wettest place on earth. Gets more rain than anywhere else. That's why you'll almost always see clouds around the peak."

"It's spectacular," she breathed.

On the way to the far side of the island, Lani pointed out various sights to his enthralled passenger. "Did you know that Mark Twain visited here once?"

"Mark Twain?"

"Yep. He called Waimea the Grand Canyon of the Pacific." Then he nodded out the window, towards fields. "Have you noticed the different cane fields?"

"Some are short. Others are tall. Some are yellowed, like they're dying. Those have a flowery top, similar to corn."

"Give the lady a gold star. The withered cane with the flowery top is ready for burning."

"Burning? I thought they harvested it."

"They burn the fields to get rid of the foliage. Then they harvest the stalks, to make sugar."

"You're quite good at being a tour guide." Sarah tried to take in everything at once. "This is much more interesting than when I was here before. Of course, everyone was too busy to show me around."

"When was that?"

"The day after the hurricane blew in."

"Well, no wonder."

"The island doesn't look like a hurricane came through here recently, though."

"It's taken a lot of work, to get it back in shape. How long were you here then?"

"Only a couple of days. I didn't have time for much sight seeing. Then I had to leave the island to cover another story." She shook her head. "It's amazing that nature can create such devastation."

"Yeah, you're right about that. We're recovering, though. Look at those palm trees without foliage, the ones that look like tall stumps.

Sarah looked where he pointed.

"During the hurricane, the wind velocity got up to about 160 miles per hour. Most of the roofs around here are made out of tin. The wind blew the roofs off and sheared the tops off those trees like a machete. The palms will never grow back. It's going to take years for this island to fully recover. But at least I'll have a job." He grinned wickedly.

"Don't you take anything seriously?" she asked, unable to stop smiling at him.

"Only the things that are worth being serious about."

They drove up the long winding road to the canyon. Sarah and Lani spent hours hiking around the sheer cliffs, streaked with red. Periodically cars and buses drove up with sightseers, but after a while would leave again. Helicopters buzzed around the steep cliffs like giant flies, showing tourists the breath-taking view from above.

"That would be wonderful," she said, pointing to the helicopters, out of breath from their climb.

"A friend of mine flies one of those, if you're interested."

"I'd love it."

"Good. I'll call him soon. Come on, let's go." He held his hand out to help her down, but she scrambled down the incline on her own.

Then he drove them down to the ocean.

She took off her sandals and walked barefoot on the warm sand, squiggling it between her toes. "This beach is a lot cleaner than L.A.'s"

"We intend to keep it that way."

"You talk like an environmentalist."

"I am. In fact, I work for the state, making sure Kauai stays like this."

Sarah smiled ironically. "I had the idea you do stand-up comedy for a living."

"No, actually I'm quite a thoughtful guy when it comes to my island."

"Why do you call it your island?"

"Because if I don't take care of her, I'm afraid other people will destroy her."

They walked along a while in silence.

Then Sarah caught sight of a dark stain on the horizon. "What's that?'

"Ni'ihau. It's the only island that still belongs completely to the Hawaiians."

"Why don't you live there?"

"I can't. You have to be full-blooded Hawaiian to even go there, and I've got some haole blood in me, a Mormon preacher I'm told."

"What's howlee?"

"Oh, that's Hawaiian for white people. I've never seen pictures of Ni'ihau, but I'm told the people live like they did hundreds of years ago. No TV or cars. Not even electricity or running water."

"How do they make a living?"

"Mostly off the land, growing taro and fishing. Living like our ancient ancestors. And the women make Ni'ihau shell jewelry, which we sell for them on the other islands. They're beautiful. The jewelry, I mean." He quickly added, "Well, the women too, I guess."

Sarah studied Lani's face. When he talked about Hawaii and all things Hawaiian, his face glowed with pride and love. "How many people live there? On Ni'ihau?" She stumbled over the pronunciation.

"Oh, about three hundred or so." His face got a pinched look and he scowled. "They're all that's left of hundreds of thousands of people."

"That seems to be the fate of indigenous people everywhere."

"I don't live everywhere. I live here," he replied curtly. His face became dark and unreadable.

She changed the topic. "You really love it here."

"Yeah." He took a deep breath and his expression lightened immediately. "The island isn't just my home. It's my blood, my roots, my family. My one true love."

"You make it sound like a woman."

"She's the only woman who'll let me live my life the way I want to. She takes up most of my time. But here and there I've found time for other interesting women." His tone was joking and his dimples cut deeply into his face again.

"Interesting?" she said with emphasis.

"Yeah, interesting." He pretended to look away, but in reality was enjoying teasing her immensely.

"But no one special?" She was on a fishing expedition, but didn't care if he knew it.

"Nope. I'm a bachelor and probably always will be."

Warning lights flashed inside Sarah. Yet she persisted. "What if you met the right woman?"

"Mmmm, dunno." He slipped off his shoes and walked down to the water's edge. "Okay. That's enough interviewing. How about you?"

"What about me?"

"Don't act coy. It doesn't suit you. Have you found anybody special?"

"A few." She waited for his reaction and wasn't disappointed.

"A few?"

"I keep them for a while, then throw them back. Depends on the size of the catch." She grinned at him and he realized she was joking in return.

"Score one for you."

Sarah changed the subject. "Where can I find your Ni'ihau shells? They sound lovely."

He stretched, brushing her side with his hand as he did so. Sarah wasn't sure if he did it by accident or had planned the move.

Come on," he said, bending down to scoop up his shoes. "There's a great little store near here that advertises the best prices on the island."

"Oh, good. I'm dying to shop."

Lani drive to a small building, a hut really, where an older Polynesian woman had arranged many pieces of shell jewelry for sale.

After looking around, Sarah picked out a triple strand shell lei, with brown, light red, and cream colored shells. "These aren't cheap." She showed him the price tag.

"No, it takes a lot of work to make one necklace. Foraging the beach for shells every day. Sorting. Stringing. Very valuable."

She paid the older woman in cash and cautiously fastened the necklace around her neck.

"Looks pretty on you, especially against your white dress."

She fingered the delicate shell necklace lovingly.

"It's getting late. Are you hungry?"

"Starved."

"I know a great place that serves luau chicken. The ambiance isn't much, but the food is delicious." He took her to what was little more than a diner, with linoleum floors, plastic flowers in a vase, and paper napkins. But he was right about the taste.

Sarah licked her fingers. The plate in front of her was soon piled with bones. "This chicken is fantastic."

"I told you. More?"

"No. I'm stuffed." She finished the last of her steamed rice. "What's their recipe?"

"Generally, it's a well-guarded island secret. But you can taste the fresh ginger, soy sauce, sugar, and pineapple juice. I'm not sure what else."

After their supper they went back to a nearby beach to watch the sun set over Ni'ihau.

Lani brought out some grass mats for them to sit on. As they watched, the sky turned psychedelic shades of reds, pinks, lavenders, and purples. Sarah leaned back against his chest, her body tucked naturally between his legs, her head resting on his shoulder, as both enjoyed the mild evening breeze. "You're lucky to be born here. Live here. I probably sound corny, but Kauai is so beautiful, it makes me want to cry."

"I feel that way a lot. I can't imagine anyone wanting to live anywhere else."

Sarah's hair floated around her like a light coppery red veil, blowing into Lani's face. He lightly touched the shell necklace, grazing her skin with his fingers. Then he closed his eyes, feeling her warm body, smelling her perfume in the soft tresses and luxuriating in the sensations. In his mind's eye, he imagined them naked on the sand. In the vision, Sarah knelt over him, her long hair gliding up and down his body, caressing his bare quivering skin with its soft filaments.

"It's a huge canvas, and a giant artist is sweeping different colors onto it with his brush," she mused about the sunset, interrupting his fantasy, drawing pictures with her finger in the sky. She stood up and brushed the sand off. "I'm going to get my camera out of the car. I have to capture this."

"Let me." He brought the camera back to her and she took a number of photos before the sky's colors faded. "Every evening the sky is different. And spectacular." He stroked her bare arm with his fingers.

"Mmmmm," she murmured.

"Look at those waves," he said, pointing to the breakers. "I wish I had brought my surf board."

"You surf?"

"Yeah."

"Is it hard to do?"

"It takes a lot of practice. Guess it's a little late for it today, though."

Darkness began to fall and they went back to his black SUV. Night came quickly after dusk at this latitude.

Lani drove her back to Opeakaa Falls to get her car. Neither of them talked much on the return trip.

Sarah reclined her seat and closed her eyes, another headache threatening. She knew when they had returned to the falls, because she could hear the loud roar of the water plummeting into the valley.

Lani pulled up next to her car and turned off the headlights. Then he got out and opened her door. He lounged against the driver's side of Sarah's rental car, so she was unable to get in.

Without streetlights or houses nearby, the scenic spot was engulfed in inky blackness. Myriads of stars brilliantly lit up the night sky. The moon hadn't risen yet, so Sarah couldn't see Lani's face. His voice was clearly audible in the dark, however.

"Did you enjoy my tour?" he asked quietly.

"Very much," she replied, trembling, goose bumps forming on her skin. Was it the cooling air or something else?

"I could take you to see the north side tomorrow. If you want to, that is," he added quickly. "I live there, in Hanalei. It's even more beautiful than what I've already showed you. But I'm prejudiced."

Her thoughts began to spin, and she tried to think clearly. But the fragrance of the plumeria nearby, with Lani standing close to her, was dizzying. She could feel the heat of his body. The force of the waterfall matched the energy flowing between them. She forced herself to talk, to break the spell. "After breakfast?"

"Before. After. It's Sunday. I have the whole day off." Lani reached out his right hand and guided it under her long, thick hair until it came to rest on her warm neck below her ear.

Sarah was breathing harder, acutely aware of his touch. She shifted towards him, chewing her lip slightly, suddenly shy.

Without moving his hand, he stroked her face with his thumb.

She closed her eyes involuntarily.

"You're quite an Amazon," he whispered. "Almost as tall as me." He grazed her mouth with his lips. Then he lightly kissed her cheek, her eyes, her forehead, teasing her.

Hungrily, Sarah found herself searching for his lips. She took his face in her two slender hands, and made contact, leaning against him, then kissed his full sensuous lips deeply, strongly.

His probing tongue found her mouth and she opened it. Lani stroked her legs and hips through the short thin dress, kissing her for a long time.

She could feel the naked skin of his thighs against hers. Rhythmically, their bodies undulated in unison, as they kissed.

Suddenly Sarah felt quite dizzy and broke the contact, put her head against his shoulder, breathing heavily. A stab of pain shot through the front of her head and her legs buckled under her. "Oh, dear."

Lani caught her before she could fall.

"Sorry," she muttered, holding her head with her hand.

"What's the matter?" He tried to look at her face, but couldn't see anything in the darkness.

"I have a headache. Nothing serious," she lied. "I must be tired from our tour." She pulled away, bracing her head with her hand. "I think I better get back to my hospital."

"Your what?"

She laughed nervously. "I mean my hotel. Thank you for a wonderful day. I really enjoyed it." She kissed him gingerly on the cheek, every movement of her head now an agony.

"Don't mention it." He sounded annoyed. Then Lani stepped away from her car, letting her unlock the door. "Where are you staying?"

"The Poipu Sheraton. Room 1211"

"I'll come get you at 9:00. Is that too early?"

"No, that's fine."

"See you then."

He jumped in his black SUV and drove away so fast that the tires kicked up gravel from the parking lot, flinging it behind him.

Sarah got into the car, her lips tight with annoyance, and rolled down the window. Leaning against the steering wheel, she hoped she would feel better soon. Her headache pounded and throbbed with an intensity she hadn't felt before. She slowly drove back to her room, holding her head with one hand and driving with the other. Irritability and confusion about Lani's abrupt change of attitude replaced her earlier exhilaration. The bruising headache was all that was left. She undressed, fell into bed without showering, and slept fitfully.

That night she had another disturbing dream. She saw herself standing at the ocean's edge, watching the ebb and flow. A lei made of white flowers floated in the foam. The water pounded the shore in a cruel, relentless rhythm.

Lying abandoned on the beach was a small baby. The child's tears were like the ocean waves, which flowed saltily from the tiny eyes.

She woke up briefly in the middle of the night, feeling melancholy. Fortunately, the headache had abated. Then she went back to sleep and slept peacefully until morning.

Chapter 3

Exposure

Sarah had showered and dressed, and was waiting outside with a canvas bag when Lani came to pick her up. He didn't smile as she got in his car, and she missed seeing his dimples.

"How ya doing?" he asked, without sounding like he really wanted to know.

"Fine," was her short reply. She could feel a cold chill, even though the windows were open and the air was a balmy seventy-eight degrees.

As he drove rather too fast out of the driveway, she asked him, "What's the matter, Lani?"

"Nothing. I'm fine. Why?"

"You seem kind of distant."

"I guess I stepped over some kind of invisible boundary last night." His teeth were clenched and she could see his jawbone tightly etched under his skin.

"What are you talking about?"

"You mean you don't remember?"

"Remember what, Lani?" Her voice cracked. She was feeling very confused and a little agitated.

"Just forget it." But sotto voce he muttered, "If you're planning on dumping me, let me know, and I'll leave first."

"What did you say?"

"Nothing," he retorted, with a forced casualness.

"Stop the car," she demanded.

The car screeched as he pulled over to the sandy shoulder of the road.

"And turn off the engine."

Lani did as she requested. He started whistling to himself. Tapping the steering wheel with a finger. Avoiding looking at her. Staring at the traffic going by instead.

In the passenger seat Sarah was fuming. "Are you talking about when you kissed me?"

"Let's just drop it, okay?" He didn't turn his head as he replied.

"No. I don't want to drop it."

"Have it your own way."

"Lani, please look at me."

He turned his body and lay his arm up on the headrest behind her, and slid down in his seat,. But the nonchalant gesture was contradicted by his eyes. They looked rebellious and surly, even more slitted than the day before and showed his only slightly veiled irritation.

"I had a wonderful day yesterday," she began hoarsely, trying to keep her voice from shaking. *I don't know what is wrong with me*, she thought.

"You said that last night."

"Well, I meant it. But…" She didn't know how to continue the conversation, especially with the look of mistrust on his face.

"But…" he encouraged her.

"I don't mean but… I mean. God, I don't know what I mean.

"Can I start the car?"

"No, not yet." She tried to collect her thoughts.

He drummed his fingers on the backrest.

"Look!" she raised her voice, irritated now. "I don't know why you're treating me like this. I thought we were getting along really well. I like you. I liked kissing you. But then for some reason you got mad at me." She breathed an exasperated sigh. "I don't understand," she finished lamely.

"You're just like every other woman," he announced. "Give a guy mixed messages." Yet inwardly he repeated her phrase to himself, *I liked kissing you.*

"How dare you compare me…" she started.

He interrupted her. "You get a guy heated up, kissing, and touching him. But then you do the 'I've got a headache number,' and it's all over. At least I found out what you're like before…" He left the rest of his sentence unspoken.

Sarah stared at him with her mouth wide open, unbelieving. "I can't believe this!" She was talking loudly.

"Me neither," he mumbled.

"You completely misinterpreted me. I did get a headache last night. They come and go pretty violently, because I…" She stopped abruptly, realizing that she had said more than she intended to. Then, completely out of character, Sarah Arlington began to cry. Not just a few little tears, but frenzied sobs that shook her whole body, taking them both by surprise. All the pent up fear and frustration that she had been withholding for the last few weeks burst out of her.

Immediately, Lani repented. "Don't cry, Sarah." He was sitting straight up now, looking at her with compassion and a little guilt. He tentatively touched her cheek, wiping away her tears. "Please. I'm really sorry. I don't know what came over me. I'm usually pretty easy-going. But something snapped in me last night and I felt…I don't know how to explain it." He touched her arm with his hand. "I believe you, but please don't cry. I'm just a jerk."

"No," she said, grabbing his hand, and holding it tightly. "You're not a jerk. Well, maybe a little." She smiled with just the corners of her mouth, tears sparkling on her cheeks.

And Lani smiled also, dimpling in his charming way. "Forgive me?"

"Yes, I forgive you." She sniffled. "I'm sorry I yelled at you."

"No problem. Maybe I had it coming."

She sniffed, let go of his hand, and looked through her purse for some tissue. When she found the packet, she took out some, wiped her eyes, and blew her nose. Then took out some more, and blew some more. Then she looked in the vanity mirror on the back of the SUV's sun visor. "Oh, lord, I've cried off all my makeup." She looked anxiously around, trying to determine if anyone else had seen her make a complete fool of herself.

"You look okay to me. Do you want to go back to the hotel?"

"No, that's all right. If I don't look too bad."

"Daahling, you look maaavalous," he replied jokingly.

"Oh, you," she said with a touch of sarcasm, and she poked his arm mockingly.

And then they both laughed.

Sarah breathed a deep sigh of relief, that their spat was over and no harm was done. "Friends?" she asked, holding out her hand.

"Friends." He squeezed her hand in reply and let go quickly, then started the engine and they drove on. "I see you're wearing your shell necklace."

"I didn't think you noticed."

"Of course, I did."

"When I wear it I feel as if I become part of the island, the ocean, the mountains. Like the necklace has magical properties to transform me into a native. Crazy, huh?"

"Very crazy."

She socked him playfully in the arm, harder this time.

"Ow."

"Sorry."

"No, you're not."

"Yes, I am."

"Okay, I accept your apology." For a few minutes all that could be heard was the high pitched whining of rubber on concrete.

"Do you see that?" he asked.

"What are you pointing at?"

"The mountain over there."

"I don't know…" She squinted, trying to see what he was indicating in the peak.

"It's supposed to look like Queen Victoria."

Sarah looked some more. "Oh, yeah!" she exclaimed. "I see it now."

"The old broad even has a double chin." He grinned maliciously.

She rolled her eyes. Then Sarah got more comfortable, and turned in her seat to face him, adjusting the seat belt. "So," she began, "why did my having a headache, real or imagined, bother you so much?"

"Let's put all that past us, okay? I still feel like an idiot."

"No," she replied. "I think it's important, or last night wouldn't have bothered you the way it did."

"Look, I know you're a reporter and all that. But I'm not used to anybody cross-examining me about my feelings."

Sarah felt that he was avoiding talking about something that was meaningful to him—and her. "Should I talk first?" she asked.

He shrugged.

She took his gesture as an indication to continue. She took a deep breath and plunged on. "This is very difficult for me to say." She stopped and took another breath, thinking of how to express her deepest and ugliest secret. Instead she changed her mind and said bluntly. "I have this neurotic fear of men leaving me. That's why I got so angry with you this morning. I thought you were going to run away." Her face reddened.

He glanced at her quickly and then turned his attention to the traffic. His expression was unreadable.

"My dad left us when I was a kid. He just disappeared. We never heard from him or saw him again. And he never paid any child support. My mother went to a lawyer, who tried to track him down, so she could get a divorce, but he had completely vanished."

"Talk about being a jerk."

"Yeah, he was a jerk, all right. And we both missed him a lot. I used to lie awake at night feeling angry, listening to my mother cry. And I told myself that I was never going to let a man hurt me like that."

"How old were you?"

"I was about four, but I remember making that decision. And then a few years ago, I was dating a guy I thought I was in love with."

"One of the few catches?" he kidded.

"Right. He had bugged me for the longest time to marry him. But I was working on my career, traveling all over the place for the paper. I didn't think marriage was a good idea. I wanted him to wait a while."

"Did he?"

"Did he what?"

"Wait."

"No."

"Big jerk."

Sarah looked out the window, feeling the pain of Eric's desertion now as she hadn't before. "He left me without any explanation, no notes, nothing. I tried writing him, calling him, but he never answered the messages I left for him. The next thing I knew he was married to someone else."

"I see."

"So now I'm extra cautious."

"Can't say as I blame you."

"Does my talking help you?"

"A little." He cleared his throat and squirmed a little in his seat, adjusting his hands on the steering wheel. "I got left, too. My parents were killed in a boating accident and my grandparents raised me."

"I'm so sorry, Lani" she replied, putting her soft hand on his muscular arm. She felt a familiar zap of electricity. "When did that happen?" she asked, trying to ignore the feeling and to concentrate on what he was saying.

"I must have been about eight. So I went to live in a small house with five older sisters, several aunts and, of course, my grandmother." He laughed. "The only men around were my grandfather and me. I was drowning in women." He got very quiet.

"Go on," she prompted him.

"That's it."

"I don't see how that fits with last night."

"Look, there's the Coco Palms Hotel."

They drove past the hurricane-shattered resort. The windows were still boarded up. Wire cordoned off the parking lot, which was filled with debris. Sarah looked back through the rear window. "Terrible."

"The hotel is still fighting with the insurance company, trying to get them to settle the damages."

She gave him a sardonic look. "A clever ploy, my dear. But it won't work. You're on the hot seat now."

"You're a quick one, I'll give you that," he admitted.

"You still haven't told me how living in a house full of women in your formative years caused you to get angry with me."

"And articulate, too." He tried to be engaging and charming, but Sarah saw right through his ruse.

"Um, hum. Go on."

"Well. I have this fear of being suffocated. By women. I have a belief that if I get really involved, I'll die," he said with a humorless laugh. "So I pick fights to ward off impending intimacy. Talk about neurotic."

Sarah became thoughtful and put her fingers to her lips, musing. "Thank you for telling me."

He continued without further assistance. "But you want to hear something weird? I didn't pick a fight with you last night because I wanted to get away. I felt…no, I feel," he said slowly, emphasizing present tense, "a deep extraordinary feeling when I'm with you. Like somehow I know you really well, even though we've just met. But I'm petrified I'll lose you. I don't know how I can lose you, when I don't even have you, but…" He broke off, having difficulty explaining his complex feelings.

She examined his face, and could see he was telling the truth. "Odd, isn't it," she said thoughtfully. "I feel the same way. Knowing you, I mean."

"And last night when I thought you were pushing me away. I couldn't stand it. I felt like I was gonna die." His neck streaked red with emotion at his confession.

Sarah listened quietly and with awe, at his long speech. Even though she didn't know the man well, she knew enough to keep silent, to savor the holy moment of intimacy between them.

"Do you know the difference between a pit bull and a woman on PMS?" he asked her without warning, turning the conversation in a completely different direction.

"No, what is the difference between a pit bull and a woman on

PMS?" she quietly replied, knowing why he was changing tactics.

"Lipstick." He laughed heartily at the inane joke. Then he blushed, realizing too late the inappropriateness of the subject.

Sarah knew this was Lani's way of getting past his embarrassment, so she didn't get angry at his apparent childishness. Instead she softly stroked his cheek, flushed beneath the brown pigment.

Lani felt gratitude at her understanding, took her hand, and gave it a quick kiss.

They drove down the highway to Hanalei in mutual silence, deep in their own private internal worlds.

Chapter 4

Mamu

Lani drove along with his left arm on the door ledge. Both their windows were rolled down and the wind blew Sarah's hair. Periodically he would glance at her. She seemed like a goddess sitting next to him, veiled in her long golden-red hair, almost unreal but very desirable. Her perfume had a pervasive, musky bouquet, reminding him of flowers he had found in the wild interior of the island. "So how did you become a reporter?" Lani asked, simply wanting to hear her voice.

Sarah breathed deeply, thinking back. "Originally I worked on the newspaper in college, and got really interested in writing about people and events." She looked out her window. "Kilauea Lighthouse." She turned to him, excited. "Can we stop there?"

"Sure," he replied, and turned the car quickly down the asphalt road to the coastline. "But it's not open today."

"That's okay. I just want to see it." She turned to him, smiling with delight, her narrow, beautiful face framed by swirling hair, her eyes gleaming in the light.

"No problem." He grinned back at her, his dimples deepening.

Sarah gazed at his face with delight. First she focused on his dimples, a boyish touch added to the finely textured skin of his masculine face. The firm, clean-shaven jaw. A well-formed, slim mustache, accentuating those dimples. The dark eyebrows with long eyelashes framing his chocolate-brown eyes. A thick crop of black, lustrous hair completed the picture.

Self-conscious of her gaze, he returned the look momentarily. She was wearing shorts and a crop top, which showed off her slender waist and long, graceful legs to perfection. He reached over and laid his warm hand on her bare leg nearest to him, while returning his attention to the narrow road. He was wearing an old pair of Vans canvas deck shoes, without socks; his foot pushed down on the gas pedal.

Sarah gasped slightly at his touch, but didn't move away from his hand. She moved closer and touched his shoulder in return.

He was wearing a black t-shirt with a large red hibiscus flower on the front. The short sleeves were rolled up, exposing his muscular biceps. They weren't bulky, like a body builder's, but had the firm contour of a swimmer's arms. He was wearing faded denim shorts, frayed at the ends from much use. Although Sarah generally preferred more elegant attire, she liked the casual sensuality of the worn shorts exposing his robust legs and solid thighs. She ran her hand along the expanse of his upper arm and shoulder.

"Don't stop," he said in a joking manner.

Sarah had no intention of stopping. She found the sensation of steely muscle beneath smooth skin exhilarating. She could smell the faint redolence of his aftershave. The lighthouse was forgotten for the moment. She twirled a short lock of his wiry black hair between her fingers.

"Here we are," Lani said.

Reluctantly she moved her hand and got out of the vehicle. They were parked at the closed gate to the road leading up to the lighthouse. A number of people were assembled, cutting the surrounding foliage.

"What's up, Eileen?" He recognized the middle-aged lady with greying hair and glasses as the President of the Oahu-based Sierra Club.

"We're spending the weekend trimming the area. It's gotten pretty overgrown, because no one has cleaned up in ages. You know. Budget cuts," and she grimaced.

"You can say that again."

She shook her head. "We're spending our own money to come over here, to help out."

"That's fantastic. Where are you all staying?"

She pointed to a pick-up loaded with sleeping bags. "Camping out."

Sarah was over at the rail, taking pictures of the lighthouse, which was several thousand yards away, at the edge of a cliff.

The woman turned to him. "Would you like me to take your picture, Lani?"

"Sure." He went over to Sarah, explained what was happening and introduced the two women. She adjusted the focus and handed her camera over to the leader of the group.

Lani stood next to Sarah and put his arm around her waist. The small hairs on his arm tickled her naked back and she wiggled. "Be still," he advised, and held her tight.

"Smile." The woman pushed her glasses up the bridge of her nose, focused and took several shots of Lani and Sarah, with the lighthouse in the background.

"Thank you very much, Eileen." Lani smiled at the woman, dimples flaring.

The matron seemed quite taken with the younger man, and obviously enjoyed his appreciative look. "No problem, my dear," she replied warmly, and handed the camera to him.

"Yes, thank you," and Sarah also smiled at the Sierra Club President.

The woman smiled at her in return, secretly envying Sarah's being with the handsome Hawaiian. Then the lady rejoined the others, who were energetically hacking away at the overgrown brush and shrubs.

Ordinarily Sarah would have been curious, stopping to ask the woman her usual kinds of questions. But today she was distracted by the attractive, friendly islander whom she hardly knew, traveling together in intimate proximity.

After touring outside the lighthouse, as Lani drove through the town of Kileaua, they passed a tiny stone church with a distinctive pointed steeple. The churchyard was overrun by flowers, ferns, and elephant ears.

"That's lovely," she exclaimed. "Slow down. I want to get some pictures."

He parked by the side of the road and they got out to inspect the old building closer.

"Except for the roof, it came through several hurricanes intact. They removed the stained glass panels, to protect them from the wind, then reinstalled them."

"Is it very old?"

"Yes, quite old. One of the original missionaries had it built. Here's a plaque showing the date." He picked up several soda pop cans that were lying in the grass. "Why don't people clean up after themselves?"

She zoomed in on the worn iron sign. "What a romantic church."

"Um, hm," and he guided her back to the car without further comment, throwing the cans behind the driver's seat on the floor of the SUV.

Once back on the main road, Lani and Sarah chatted about the people they had just met and the continuing clean-up of the island.

They had only traveled a mile or two when Lani pulled off the road next to a large fruit stand. "I'll be right back. Don't go away."

"I promise."

When he returned he had a large plate full of cut-up fresh pineapple slices and papaya, along with some coconut chips. "Breakfast." He handed her some paper napkins. "Here, hold these. Let's sit out here." He indicated a picnic table, and she went over and sat down. Then he climbed onto the seat next to her.

"Mmmm," she mumbled, eating a piece of pineapple, while juice dribbled down her chin.

Lani chuckled. "I can dress you up but I can't take you anywhere," he mocked her, tenderly wiping off her chin with a napkin.

Her mouth was too full to reply. She smacked her lips in obvious enjoyment of the succulent tropical fruit, unembarrassed by her actions or his remark.

He chose a piece and popped it in his mouth. "Good," he agreed juicily.

For a few minutes, only silence prevailed, as each hungrily devoured the delicious produce.

"I'm all sticky," and Sarah went into the restroom to wash up.

Lani carefully threw all the trash in the garbage can provided, then followed suit. Soon they were on their way again.

"How far is it?"

"About twenty minutes."

She settled back and watched the scenery go by. Several times they passed more waterfalls, just off the road. She turned her head around quickly as they drove by. "I had no idea that Kauai was so rural."

"That's part of her charm," he smiled.

"Very charming," she agreed.

After a few more curves in the road, having made their way down a steep hill, they crossed an old iron bridge, just wide enough for one vehicle. A line of cars waited on the other side as they progressed over the bridge.

Then all at once they were in the little town of Hanalei, appearing like a mirage out of the green jungle.

The town consisted of a number of small, older stores and restaurants with tin roofs, and two small modern strip malls. A varied assortment of well-made houses and tiny huts lined the main street. Many of the homes were built on tall pilings, with a long stairway up to the main living quarters.

"Why are the houses built like that?" Sarah pointed out the tall homes.

"To protect them from the ocean. A few years ago we had a tidal wave that wiped out most of the homes here. So now they build them high off the ground. Many were protected from the hurricane because of that."

"I'd hate to lug groceries up those stairs, though," she commented.

As they passed through the main part of the small town, Sarah saw another old church, with a number of smaller buildings and a school on the large mission grounds.

Everywhere, around the stores, houses and mission grounds, flowers bloomed, while trees, ferns and other tropical plants thrived in profusion. The foliage had to be constantly trimmed back to keep the yards looking civilized.

A number of shops boasted surf board rentals, snorkel equipment, and kayaks for paddling up the Hanalei river.

"What a magnificent town!" Sarah exclaimed, craning her neck to see everything at once. She saw several specialty stores she wanted to browse through, but Lani drove on. "Oh," she said, with disappointment.

"We'll come back later. Right now I want to show you my favorite places. There's one over there."

She looked to where he was pointing. She saw a group of low mountains, with one lone black ridge sticking out.

"Did you ever see the old movie South Pacific?"

"Of course. Mitzi Gaynor. Rossano Brazzi."

"Well, that's Bali Hai."

She gazed at the promontory, remembering scenes from the movie. Unconsciously, she began quietly singing the words to the song. "Bali Hai, my little island. Come to me. Come to me." She stopped singing, thinking of the tragic love story between the American sailor and the Tonkinese girl, suddenly a little melancholy.

"Nice voice," he commented.

"Thanks," she replied softly.

After they left Hanalei, they drove over a series of narrow bridges. Lani explained, "These were originally built for sugar cane wagons."

He pulled into a sandy parking lot, near a beach. They scrambled out of the vehicle and briefly explored the dry cave across the street. In the tomb-like cavern, Sarah called out "Bali Hai," and her words echoed back to her. Then they got back into the vehicle.

"There's one more place I want to show you." A few minutes later he parked again. He pointed to a ridge. "We're going to hike up there. It's not a difficult climb. There's a special heiau at the top I want to show you."

Lani was accurate in his description. The short hike was easy; the path well-marked. At the top, in a clearing, was another circle of black stones. "This is the Hula Heiau, sacred to dancers. We're allowed inside this one." He held her hand and helped her over the three-foot wall of black lava rocks. The circle was much wider than the other one near Opeakaa Falls, and Sarah didn't feel the tingling she had felt there. Nor did she hear any internal chanting.

She wandered around. On the summit, the wind was blowing hard, and she loved the feel of the sea air buffeting her body around. Below them was the ocean, the waves colliding noisily against the rocky shore. "I feel wild and free," she shouted to him. She twirled around and around like a little girl, giggling to herself, until she started to get dizzy.

Lani was sitting on the embankment of stones, watching her, grinning. "I knew you'd like it."

"What did you say?" she called. "I can't hear you."

But he just waved her off.

She kicked off her shoes and danced around, laughing. Every once in awhile, she picked up a pebble and flung it at him, waiting to see his reaction. After the third or fourth time she did that, he got up and dashed over to her.

Sarah ran around the inside of the ring of sacred stones, Lani in pursuit. She had a head start, but he was more athletic. At last he caught up to her, enveloping her from behind, crossing his arms in front of her. They each had red faces, were breathing hard and laughing at the same time.

She pulled away and ran to the stony enclosure, climbed over it and began the descent down the hill. "Last one down's a rotten egg!" she yelled to him. She was waiting at the bottom when he finally jogged down to her.

"What took you so long?"

"You forgot your shoes." He handed them to her and opened the door.

"Thanks." She flung herself inside. "I haven't had so much fun since I was a kid," she said breathlessly.

Her face was grimy and her hair disheveled, but to Lani she was lovely. He leaned over to kiss her mouth, but she was still giggling, so he kissed the tip of her nose instead. "Have you ever tried snorkeling?" he asked, starting the engine.

"Once or twice," she replied.

"I know a beach just a few minutes from here. One of the best places on the island to snorkel."

"Okay."

"Did you bring a suit?"

"In here," and she pointed to her canvas bag.

Within minutes, they had arrived at the uninhabited beach, changed into their swimsuits, and were down at the water's edge. Lani had brought some snorkeling gear with him and they were putting the fins on, and adjusting their masks. He waded like a duck through the waves and turned to see where Sarah was. She stood frozen at the edge of the water.

"Come on in," he motioned. "The surf's real calm today."

But she shook her head, "No, I can't."

Lani came back to where she stood at the beach's end, staring into the vastness of the ocean, with a look of terror on her face. A few migrant tears had wandered down her cheeks.

"What's the matter, honey?" This was the first time he had used an endearing phrase with her.

"It's so...big, and uncaring."

"What is?"

"That," she replied, pointing to the sea.

"I used to be afraid of it, too. When I was a baby, they tell me. Can you imagine? A Hawaiian afraid of water." He joked with her to make her feel better.

She talked slowly, as if in a dream. "I don't know what the matter is with me. I haven't been myself since I got to this island." Her eyes were unblinking as she spoke, as if hypnotized.

"Do you want to go back to the car?"

"No, I'm okay." She shook herself a little. "The last few days I act like a different person, with feelings that I don't understand." She adjusted her mask again. "I'm okay now," and she waddled awkwardly into the water.

He followed her and they both swam out a few hundred feet. Sarah was a strong swimmer and Lani of course was in his accustomed element.

The rocks and coral below were habitation to a number of brightly colored fish, large and small. Sarah and Lani floated on the surface of the water, looking down at the fish through their masks, breathing through the snorkel tubes. On the ocean floor, the sand swished back and forth, as the waves came in and withdrew out to sea again.

Fish swam confidently through the currents. Periodically Sarah would reach out to touch one of the large silver fish that was hovering nearby, but it always swam out of reach.

Lani was amused as each time she attempted to touch one of the fish, it propelled itself further away from the woman's hands with a quick flip of its fins, intuiting her movement. The childish look of delight on her face as she toyed with the fish endeared her to him.

Lani looked at his underwater watch and raised his head out of the water. They had been snorkeling, observing the movements of fish for almost an hour and the current was getting stronger, with an undertow that was moving them further out to sea. The waves had gotten rougher, too. He removed his mouthpiece. "We should be heading in," and motioned to Sarah to follow him.

When they got to shore, Lani had taken off his fins and was waiting for her. Sarah was standing in front of him, with her back to the water, when a large wave knocked her over. Like a runaway bowling ball, she collided with Lani, and they were swept up the beach, jumbled together, choking on the salt water. He pulled her further in before another wave could wash over them, and lay on the beach, gasping and laughing.

But Sarah only grabbed the back of her head, wrinkling up her forehead as she did so, in obvious pain. She tried to stand up, but the fins made her clumsy and she fell down on the sand. "Oh, not again!"

Lani put his arms around her, and she collapsed into his smooth chest, moaning. He looked around the beach but it was deserted, so he quickly formulated a plan. First he removed both of their fins and masks, throwing them on the sand. Then he gathered her up in his arms. "Hold on to me," he said, and he strode through the sand to where his car was parked. "Can you stand up?"

"I think so."

He set her down gently.

"I'm seeing two of everything." She looked around dazed. He could see distress in her eyes.

"That fall really hurt you."

She shook her head. "I'll be okay. Just let me sit for a minute."

He opened the door and she got in.

Lani noticed that her legs were trembling. "I'm going to retrieve our equipment. Will you be all right until I get back?"

She nodded her head, then her face contorted as pain ripped through her skull.

The tall Hawaiian literally ran down the beach, scooped up the snorkel gear and ran back again. "I'm going to take you to the hospital."

"No!" Sarah exclaimed. Trying to reassure him and herself, she continued. "I'll be fine. I just need to rest a bit."

Then he climbed in the vehicle, started the engine, and with a rush, drove off. "I'm going to take you to my grandfather's house, then. It's close. You're not going to pass out or anything, are you?"

"No, silly," and she made a brave face. But internally Sarah was frightened, dizzy, and sick to her stomach. She lay back against the seat, trying not to show how scared she was.

When Lani arrived at his family house, he drove into the makeshift driveway, frightening several chickens from the front yard, which flapped away with a great squawk. Sarah noticed the paint was old and peeling from the wooden structure, which sagged somewhat on its raised concrete block foundation. Lani rushed around to her door, and helped Sarah out.

"I'm much better," she replied to his unspoken question, but she slumped a little.

He held her arm, helping her walk up the steps to the battered screen door, the material torn from the wood and flapping in the breeze.

A massive, elderly Hawaiian woman pushed it open for them.

"Gramma, this is Sarah. Sarah, this is my grandmother."

"Hello, Sarah. I'm glad to meet you."

Sarah just nodded.

"Is it okay if she lies down on your bed? She's not feeling very good," he explained.

""Of course, Lani. Too much sun, honey?" she asked in a melodious voice. She patted Sarah on the shoulder consolingly. "Lani," she said chiding him. "You shouldn't let this nice lady get sunstroke." She turned to Sarah. "He's always out surfing, surfing. Someday he'll turn into a fish. But he forgets other people aren't like him."

"I'm sorry to put you to all this trouble," Sarah said, in an apologetic voice.

"No trouble at all. Lani never brings girls home to meet us."

He cleared his throat. "Why don't you get her some something to drink, Gramma?"

"Sure. I'll be back, by and by."

Sarah could hear the floors creak as the enormous woman ambled to the kitchen.

"I can't lie on the bed, Lani. I'm all wet and covered with sand."

"Hmmm." The lanky man thought for a moment.

"Would you get my bag out of the car? Then I can shower off the sand and put dry clothes on."

"Good idea." He was off immediately and returned with her possessions. "The bathroom is just to the left."

After she had showered and dressed in dry clothes, Sarah lay down in the small bedroom.

Lani knelt by the bed, picked up her hand and held it tenderly, bringing it to his mouth, kissing her soft fingers one by one.

Sarah could feel the tingling begin again, in spite of her severe headache and dizziness.

Just then, Lani's grandmother brought in some lemonade, interrupting them.

Lani jumped to his feet, staring at the walls.

The old woman fussed over her. "More pillows? Are you warm enough, honey?" She picked up an old quilt constructed with a uniquely Hawaiian pattern and laid it over Sarah.

"Thank you. I'm fine, Mrs. uh, Why, uh…" She had forgotten how to pronounce Lani's last name.

"Why-a-ka-low-a." The large woman smiled pleasantly, showing several teeth missing, as she patiently enunciated the syllables with a deep voice, almost sounding as if she were singing.

"Mrs. Waikoloa. I'm afraid I'm being a bother."

"You don't worry about that. Now, you lay back. Relax. If you need anything, I'll be out in the kitchen."

Lani grinned at Sarah when the large woman left. His smile was similar to his grandmother's, except that all his gleaming white teeth were intact. "I wanted you to meet my family eventually. I didn't realize it was going to be this soon, though."

Sarah closed her eyes and tried to relax. The pain seemed like a spike driven into the middle of her forehead.

He held her hand and rubbed it absentmindedly, uncertain about what to do next.

Sarah heard the screen door open and close. Then a man's voice that was deeper than any she had ever heard asked, "Mother, are you here?"

"In the kitchen, Mamu."

"That's my grandfather," Lani whispered.

"The Kahuna?" asked Sarah, her eyes getting big. "He sounds like thunder."

"That's what I thought, too, when I was a kid. His voice used to scare me, but he's the kindest person you could ever meet."

"Some lemonade, my honey man?" she asked her husband affectionately.

"Thank you, my dear. Is that Lani's car?"

"You know it is."

"Where is he?"

"In the front bedroom. She don't feel so good."

"Who?"

"Lani's friend." She whispered loudly, emphasizing the word "friend."

Sarah squeezed Lani's hand for protection as she heard the man coming down the hall. When the shaman appeared in the doorway, she half-expected him to be wearing a loincloth, shells around his neck, and a feathered headdress. To her amazement he wore old, baggy Levi's, a faded red-and-white plaid shirt with the sleeves rolled up, and a perspiration-stained baseball cap.

Sarah had never before seen a person with as many wrinkles as Lani's grandfather. Time had eroded deep lines and gullies in his skin. But his eyes twinkled with an incredible intelligence and aliveness rarely seen in someone half his age.

"What's going on here?" the old man asked gruffly. "Hello, young lady." He inspected her face closely, adjusting his bifocals.

"Grandfather. I'd like you to meet a friend of mine, Sarah Arlington. Sarah, this is my…"

He interrupted. "Pleasure to meet you, Sarah Arlington." He shook her hand and his eyes sparkled with the pleasure he truly felt. Then he smiled, and the criss-crossed lines in his right cheek formed an unusual star-shaped pattern. He patted her hand before relinquishing it, and said to his grandson, "She is very pretty. I hope you don't go breaking her heart."

Lani spoke up quickly. "Please, grandfather…"

The old man interrupted again, with his low-pitched voice. "I know. I'll try not to embarrass you. But if you're not careful, I will steal her myself." The old man chuckled.

Sarah blushed deep red. "I'm glad to meet you, Mr. Waikoloa." She said the syllables slowly but correctly. "Lani has told me a lot about you." She tried not to stare at his cheek, but forced herself to look into his eyes instead.

"Oh, he has?" grinned the ancient Kahuna. "Don't believe half of what he says."

Now I can see where Lani gets his humor, thought Sarah. She felt greatly relieved and more at ease with the old gentleman.

"What seems to be the problem?"

Lani spoke up. "We were snorkeling and she fell down. I think she might have hit her head, maybe got a concussion. Her head hurts, she's been dizzy, and a little while ago she was seeing double."

Before Sarah could protest, the Kahuna put his leathery hand on her head.

"Oh!" she cried with surprise.

The whole house shook as Lani's grandmother lumbered down the hall, crowding her bulk into the tiny room, her long, vast dress flapping like a tent around her.

"Mamuhiwahiki!" she scolded him. "What do you think you're doing, scaring that girl?"

"Shhh, old woman. I'm trying to concentrate." He had closed his eyes, and seemed to be in a trance.

Sarah felt warmth emanating from his hand, which grew hotter the longer he left it on her head. She closed her eyes, too. The heat was soothing and her body relaxed. The old Kahuna kept his hand on her head for a few minutes, while Sarah lost track of time. She felt as though she was drifting, floating on a serene, blue ocean, while fish swam beneath her, tickling her with their fins. She felt happy, loved, and safe. Then she sensed death was stalking her in the murky depths of the water. Abruptly she opened her eyes as he removed his hand.

Grandfather Mamu was studying her with a stern expression. His face no longer looked pleased; the star on his cheek had disappeared. He glanced at Lani, then back at Sarah again. Without another word, he got up and went into the kitchen, followed by his wife.

Sarah could hear the Kahuna's deep voice murmuring quietly, as Mr. and Mrs. Waikoloa discussed her. Then the screen door opened and closed and the thunderous voice was gone.

Lani had watched the unfolding of the whole scene with Sarah and his grandfather, and was frankly baffled. But he did sense that his grandfather knew something important and wasn't talking.

Lani went into the kitchen. "Did Grandfather tell you what he sensed from Sarah?" he asked his grandmother.

"She doesn't have a concussion."

"Well, that's good news."

The large woman shrugged.

He went back to the small bedroom. Sarah had gotten up and was brushing her damp, tangled hair in front of an antiquated mirror; in places the silver had rubbed off.

"Do you think you should walk around?"

"I'm much better. No, really I am," she added, seeing his doubtful expression. "Whatever your grandfather did made the headache go away completely."

"Good. I never argue with my grandfather." He reconsidered, then laughed. "Well, hardly ever." He handed her the canvas bag. "If you're up for it, I'll take you to dinner. I know a restaurant nearby that serves wonderful mahimahi. Made with shredded coconut, soy sauce, honey, and lots of macadamia nuts."

"Say no more. I'm ready." She looked down at her outfit. "But I didn't bring anything to wear."

"You look fine. Casual is always in style here."

"If you say so."

"I'm all sweaty, though. I'll be back in a couple of minutes."

Sarah heard the screen door slam and after she had finished her hair, she wandered into the fragrant kitchen. Several pots were cooking on the old porcelain stove, steam making the lids dance and rattle. "What smells so good?" she inquired of the old woman.

"Just rice, chicken, and vegetables," she answered, with a gaping smile. Droplets of sweat trickled down the old face, which was smoother than her husband's. She wiped her face with the back of a plump hand. "There's plenty. Why don't you sit down and I'll serve you some?"

"Oh, no thank you," Sarah replied politely. "I think we're going out for dinner."

"Hummmp," was the woman's only reply. She turned and cautiously removed a lid from one of the cooking pots. Vapor shot up, released from its captivity. She unscrewed the top of a small glass bottle and sprinkled some of its yellowish contents into the pot. She added some coconut chunks and raisins, pieces of fresh ginger from a well-worn cutting board, stirring the pot vigorously. Then she replaced the lid, wiping her hands on the front of her dress. "How long have you known my Lani?" the old woman asked.

"Two days," replied Sarah.

"Two days!?" the old woman repeated, incredulous.

"It seems like a lot longer…somehow." Sarah's voice trailed off.

"I got the impression you were close…friends." The Hawaiian woman seemed puzzled.

"Um, no." Sarah stopped, unwilling to explain how they had met, embarrassed at the unusual circumstances.

"He seems quite fond of you. In fact, I've never seen my Lani act so sweet around any girl before."

"Oh, really?"

"And you're the first haole he ever brought home."

"Haole?"

"That word means a stranger. A white person. Not an islander."

"Oh, yeah." Sarah blushed so profoundly that she could feel the heat rise under her hair.

The native woman was instantly flustered. "Oh, dear. I didn't mean…I'm not prejudiced…" She gripped her hands together. "Lani will be furious at me. I'm always saying the wrong things. Please forgive me."

"That's okay, Mrs. Waikoloa," Sarah hastened to reassure the Hawaiian woman.

"No, it's not okay. I want you to know I didn't mean anything bad. I can tell Lani likes you a lot. And you seem like a good person." She stammered, trying to explain herself.

Sarah touched the woman's plump hand. "I understand, honestly. I guess Lani and I just hit it off right away. And somehow I feel like I belong here on this island."

"Sometimes haoles come to the island. They believe the same thing. We call them white Hawaiians. Maybe that's what you are." She took a deep breath and sat down on a wooden kitchen chair, which groaned ominously.

Before the embarrassed woman could say anything more, Lani appeared. He had quickly showered, then changed into a pair of white cotton slacks and an aloha shirt. The colorful shirt had green, blue, and red parrots on a white background, unbuttoned at his neck. The white shirt made his brown skin look darker and his soft black hair gleamed.

"Where did you get clothes?" asked Sarah, believing that he was as mysterious as his grandfather.

"Over there." He pointed to the kitchen window. Outside, beyond the old chintz curtains she could see other small houses behind his grandparents'. "This is our family's land," he indicated with a wave of his hand. He noticed the strained look on his grandmother's face. "What's the matter, Gramma?"

"Nothing. I'm fine."

"Are you sure?"

The elderly woman looked at Sarah, smiled conspiratorially, and shook her head. "All okay," she assured him.

"Are you two keeping secrets from me?"

"Secrets?" Sarah replied innocently, but grinning.

He decided to let it go. "My house is over there."

Sarah saw a small, white cottage, which desperately needed paint. "How wonderful, and close to the beach, too."

He nodded happily.

"Do your sisters live in the other houses?"

"They've all moved away. My favorite aunt still lives here, though. She's pretty old, but she works in the garden every day."

"How about the other houses?" Sarah had counted five more that she could see through the steamed-up kitchen window.

"Some of my cousins. We're a very close-knit family. Come on. I'll show you."

He took her hand and led her out into the yard through the open back door. Grass grew thinly, mixed together with weeds, both of which were trampled down by many feet. Some vegetables were growing in rows beyond the houses, mostly ones she didn't recognize. Further back were some trees, coconut and macadamia nuts. Flowers bloomed everywhere, fragrant plumerias, giant hibiscus bushes, red ginger, and birds-of-paradise. Chickens roamed around the yard, scratching in the red dirt, looking for insects. A scrawny rooster stretched his head towards them aggressively, his feathers standing up around his neck, and crowed. Satisfied, the bird strutted back to his home in the grove of banana trees near the field.

"How big is this place?"

"About twenty acres. That includes the houses, the trees, and the fields. Some of it's lying fallow right now. My cousins do most of the farming. Grandfather is too old, and I'm busy with my work."

"I'm amazed. It could be something out of a Mitchener novel."

"I'm glad you like it." He beamed with pleasure, then looked towards the light shining from the kitchen. "I'm hungry. But if we stay here much longer, grandmother will be insulted if we don't eat what she's cooked." He walked up to the kitchen door. "Bye, Gramma. We're leaving now."

The old woman gestured for him to hug her, and he was enveloped in her massive flesh. She turned to Sarah. "You come back now. Any time. You're always welcome in my house."

"Thank you for everything, Mrs. Waikoloa. Maybe next time I won't make such a commotion."

"No problem." The woman smiled warmly at her, then returned to her stove.

Lani drove back through Hanalei town.

"Your grandparents are very nice," Sarah commented.

"Thank you. They liked you a lot, too," he emphasized.

"You think so?"

"Yes, I know so."

"I was afraid I upset your grandfather. He left looking like he was mad at me."

"Grandfather has his moods, but I wouldn't worry about it. He frequently goes off by himself."

"You don't think your grandmother is unhappy because I'm a haole?"

"Did she call you that?"

"Well, yes," she admitted.

"I'm sure she didn't mean anything bad by it. I think she was just surprised by you."

"Surprised."

"Believe me, if they didn't like you, you would know it." He patted her knee. "Not that I mean they aren't kind. They are the most caring people I know, and I love them very much. They raised me after my parents died and I would do anything for them. They spoiled me rotten. I was prince of the world." He smiled, remembering.

Sarah gazed at his cheerful expression, swept up in his words.

"When I was a kid, I was forever tracking in red mud from outside. But gramma never complained. Just waited until it dried and then swept it out the door."

"I keep house like that a little," she joked.

"They always made sure we celebrated my parents' birthdays and wedding anniversary, just as if they were simply away on vacation, unable to attend. We'd get out all the family pictures and decorate them with flowers and shells. And gramma would prepare their favorite foods. We'd eat some, leave some by the photos, and take some to the heiau so the gods could bless them."

"How sweet." Sarah was enraptured over the story of his childhood.

"Whatever I wanted, my grandparents bought for me. I don't know how they afforded it. I always got to pick out my presents. They never told me something was too expensive or too silly or complained if I broke it or gave it away or got tired of it."

"I wish I had experienced that kind of acceptance in my childhood."

"When I told them I wanted to go to the university, to learn how to take care of the island, they made sure I always had the money to attend, for books, for anything I needed. I think they even sold some of the property so I could finish."

"I had to put myself through school. Worked two jobs, usually."

"I was lucky. They loved me absolutely. I guess I always wanted a woman to love me like that. No one ever has. Until now."

"Are you referring to me?"

"Of course, I mean you."

"You see me like that?" Her eyes opened wide with amazement.

"Sarah, you are like that. Gentle. Affectionate. Unconditionally loving."

"I thought I'm demanding and selfish, not to mention stubborn and willful."

"Not around me you aren't."

"Maybe I do love you like that. Most of the time. But once in a while you act arrogant," she said, poking fun at him.

"Well, it's because I'm a Leo," he grinned, ruffling up his thick black hair into a mane. "Grrrr," he roared quietly at her.

"That explains it," she giggled.

"Leo's like to be king."

"Emperor," she corrected him, still teasing.

"God," he added, and they both laughed.

Then they were once again in Kileaua, and they drove past the stone church to Lani's restaurant, which was more upscale than the one the previous day. Waiters hovered nearby. The walls were papered with straw wallpaper, with framed pictures of sailboats and sunsets hung artistically throughout. The tablecloths and napkins were starched pink linen. All tables were set with matching vases of fresh flowers.

They were seated at a table on the lanai adjacent to the backyard, screened to discourage mosquitoes. A riot of flowers and plants were flourishing everywhere outside.

"It's like dining in a tropical garden," she whispered.

"I'm glad you like it," he replied.

Sarah fidgeted in her cane plantation chair, pulling her shorts down over her thighs a bit, attempting to cover her bare legs. She draped a pink napkin over her exposed midriff, trying to look more elegant than she felt. "Are you sure I look okay?" she asked Lani.

"You're an orchid among daisies," he replied, dimpling.

"Thank you," she murmured, her face heating up from the compliment. "You have a wonderful way with words."

"Only with you," Lani answered sweetly. "Words come easily when I'm with you." He stared into her blue-green eyes with his dark chocolate-colored ones. "And words aren't always necessary."

Over dessert Lani told her, "I won't be able to see you tomorrow, Sarah. I'll be working."

"Oh." Sarah felt a twinge in her solar plexus, but ignored it. "What do you do exactly?"

"A number of different things. Tomorrow I'm flying to Honolulu to attend a big inter-island conference."

"When will you be back?"

"Probably not until late tomorrow or even the next day."

"What's the conference about?"

"How to bring more income to the islands. Sugar cane as a cash crop is losing money. The big sugar companies are taking their business to the Philippines and Taiwan, where labor is cheap. We're fighting developers from coming in and building resorts, more golf courses, that sort of thing. Or at least to try to slow them down a little."

Sarah found herself getting interested. Her reporter's innate sense of newsworthy material was stimulated. "Who are the developers?"

"Oh, no, you're not going to interview me. I'm in a sticky position as it is. My island needs money, so a lot of people want to bring in new construction. But developers could ruin the beauty of this place in a decade. I'm trying to balance the bad with the awful. As it is, some of the ocean is already badly polluted around Oahu and a lot of vegetation is gone forever."

"I didn't know that."

"Plus the fish population has severely decreased. With the local demand for fish, not to mention exporting fish to the mainland, our fishing industry is suffering."

"Trouble even in paradise."

"That's right. Nowhere is secure unless you safeguard the land and the water."

Sarah found herself drawn closer to this man. Even though he cracked jokes at inappropriate times and tended to avoid intimacy, she could tell that he was a caring person, involved in protecting Mother Earth and its children. "You grow more interesting with every conversation we have. You're almost as wise as your Grandfather."

"Yeah, I'm a real wise guy." He dimpled at her, with a wicked grin.

She sighed dramatically, with mock concern. "But at times you can be a wise ass."

"Hey, score one for the pretty lady with the great legs."

She hit him with her napkin. "Take me home, you cad."

He twirled what he could of his moustache and sneered. "Watch out, or I'll tie you to the railroad tracks."

"Help! Somebody save me!" she giggled.

As they left the restaurant, Lani grabbed her without warning and swung her over his shoulder, casually strolling through the parking lot to his car.

"Put me down!" she shrieked. "Lani, put me down. I can't breathe."

He set her down next to the car door, trying to stifle his laughter.

She didn't know whether she should be angry with him or not. So she punched him playfully in the arm and laughed. "You jerk."

But he only reached around her with his strong arms, pulled her to him gently and kissed her gently on her laughing mouth. She stopped laughing and kissed him back, a long, deep kiss.

They stood in the parking lot for a few minutes, wrapped in each other's embrace.

"Take me back to my hotel," she murmured.

Wordlessly, Lani opened her door, and she got in.

Then he got in his side, started the car and drove quickly back to Poipu.

Sarah turned sideways in her seat, not fastening her safety belt, so she could be closer to him. She nibbled on his ear lobe, and licked his brown neck with her tongue. Up close, she could see his skin color had reddish undertones. She unbuttoned the rest of the buttons of his shirt and reached inside. She stroked his smooth chest, letting her fingertips glide over his nipples, which stood up hard and erect. She had wanted to touch him like this since the first moment they met.

He moaned softly.

She could hear his breathing rasp in his chest.

Meanwhile, Lani stroked her upper leg as he drove, fascinated with the incredibly soft skin and solid flesh beneath his hand. He stretched his arm and reached around to her firm behind, straining to get his fingers underneath the material of her tight shorts. They each experienced delicious bursts of pleasure.

She moved her hand downward, towards his navel.

He shifted in his seat, his body subtly moving to meet her fingers. Then he stopped her hand. He was breathing very hard now. "Sarah, stop it. I can't concentrate on driving."

She laughed softly with delight.

"You like torturing me."

"Of course. But you like it too, don't you?"

"Love it. But I don't want us to have an accident. Sit back until we get there."

"Okay," she agreed reluctantly, turning in her seat. But she continued to torment him by caressing his chest periodically.

He took a sharp intake of breath. "Ah," was all he could say.

When they arrived at the Sheraton, Lani fairly leaped out of the vehicle and dashed around to her side.

"Slow down. There's no rush."

"Easy for you to say," he breathed in her ear, and he held her hand firmly.

Sarah found it difficult to walk as excitement coursed through her body. She fumbled with the key and finally got the door open.

After they had both entered the room, Lani closed the door, nudged her up against it, and began kissing her mouth, her ears, her neck, in slippery wet kisses.

He leaned his body into hers.

Sarah groaned, her body moving with its own dance.

"I've been waiting so long for this," he whispered, then kissing the soft part of her neck, where her pulse throbbed.

"But we've only known each other two days." She ran her hands through his thick, black hair, reveling in its rich texture.

"That's not what I mean," and he unzipped her shorts, sliding his hand down inside. He could feel her soft pubic hair beneath the silken panties. Then he moved his hand around to the back, still inside her shorts, to rub her bottom. "You have a great ass." He took her flesh in both hands and moved her against him.

"Thank you," she breathed softly, undulating in time to his movements.

"Every time I watch you walk in front of me, I go crazy." He kissed her on the mouth again, his tongue deep inside.

Sarah was squirming more energetically, and bumped against the door handle. "Ouch."

"Sorry." Then he took her by the hand and led her over to the king-sized bed, yanked the bedspread onto the floor, and pulled down the sheets. He slipped out of his Vans.

"I don't usually go to bed with someone this fast. Ever since I got to this island, I've been acting differently. Like I'm somebody else." She sounded apologetic.

"Don't worry. I like you, whoever you are." He unbuttoned her top and removed it, letting it drop to the floor. He slithered his fingertips over the top of her lacy bra, running them along the rounded flesh at the edge of the material. Then he unzipped her shorts and slowly slid them down her long legs. She stepped out of them.

She stood before him dressed only in her bra and panties.

Lani held her at arm's length, drinking in her beauty, his delicious dimples lighting up his handsome face. "I want to feel you under my skin, in my muscles, my blood." Then he embraced her, kissing her again. He whispered into her ear, "I want to merge with your completely. Feel our hearts beat in rhythm. Breathe in unison. Think thoughts simultaneously."

"Don't we?"

"Yes. And I want more." He held her tightly, kissing her neck and then her mouth, exploring with his tongue.

She pulled away slowly and slid her hands inside his shirt. She ran her fingers over his pectoral muscles. He flexed and the muscles jumped beneath her hands.

She squealed as he did so. Then she unzipped his white slacks and slid her hands inside them, feeling the taut skin around his navel and the curly hair below it.

Lani moaned and moved his body closer to her hands.

She smiled and teasingly moved them away. Then she slowly pulled his pants and briefs down his body, nipping at his muscular legs every few inches, until his clothes were down around his ankles.

She ran her hands up and down his powerful thighs, across his tight abdomen, around to his buttocks. Lani's body was shaking wildly with desire.

"Feels so good." He unfastened her bra, letting it fall off her shoulders, cupping her breasts in his warm hands, kissing and sucking her nipples. He reached around and squeezed her fleshy behind. Then he removed her panties, and maneuvered her onto the bed, separating her slim legs, and kneeling between them.

As he readied himself to mount her, Sarah noticed how large he was and closed her eyes expectantly.

Lani kissed her while he eased himself into her, moving slowly and deliberately, until he was completely immersed.

She groaned beneath him. "Oh, god. Oh, god."

Lani knew she wasn't praying.

He kissed her neck, then her ears, her high cheekbones.

She moaned again.

"Feel good?"

"Wonderful," she breathed. "Don't stop."

"I have no intention of stopping," he gasped.

While the ecstatic couple made love, sensations of soft ocean air billowed around them, cradling them in its gentle fragrance.

Soon after they reached a mutual climax.

The couple was perspiring but eminently satisfied.

Lani lay on top of Sarah, not wanting to move. "Too heavy?" he asked.

"You feel delicious, Lani."

After a while, Lani rolled off and lay next to her.

Sarah cuddled up to him, her head on his chest, his arm around her, enfolding her like she was a bouquet of wild flowers and they remained coupled together, their breathing slower and more regular. Soon they dozed off.

Lani woke when Sarah touched his voluptuous lips with the tip of her finger, running it over the sculpted contours of his mouth.

"Hey, that tickles." He folded his lips together.

She giggled. "Where else are you ticklish?" She tried around his ribs.

"Okay, that's enough," he said sternly, wiggling away.

"Who says?" and Sarah continued to probe around his torso.

"I say," and he gripped both of her slender hands tightly in his large one. He leaned his head over her and began nibbling on her earlobes, then put his tongue in her ear.

"Release me, you varmint," she gasped. Her ear felt all wet.

"Say the magic word."

"Please."

"Pretty please."

"Pretty please."

He let her go, turned over, and put both his hands under his head, yawning widely.

"Bored already?" she teased him.

"No. You wore me out, you wicked sex maniac. But you would never bore me."

"I'll bet you say that to all the girls."

His voice was instantly solemn. "You're the only woman I've ever said that to." Lani put his hand over her right hip. "You're so slender. My hands could fit right into your solar plexus." He slid his fingers under her ribcage to show his point.

Sarah instantly was excited and could tell he was, too. The couple made love again, only this time they did so slowly and leisurely.

When they had both reached orgasm, Sarah dropped her hands against the mattress wearily.

He kissed her taut wet belly in response and laid back on the pillow, sighing.

After a long silence, Sarah asked him. "Do you like me?"

He turned to face her. "Very much."

"I like you, too. Very much." She bit her lip. "I can't imagine why."

"Oh, thanks," he sputtered.

She continued, unabashed. "No, what I mean is, I feel really comfortable with you. Like I've known you a long time. But I haven't." She looked at her attractive lover, a tiny question mark forming in the space above the bridge of her nose. "Do you understand?"

He nodded.

"I feel like I can do anything with you. Like you belong to me."

"And you belong to me."

"Do you feel it, too?"

"It doesn't make any sense."

"No, it doesn't. After all we've only known each other..."

"...two days," he finished her sentence.

"Only two days. But you're so familiar." She laid her head on his chest, and stroked the ridges of flesh around the firm muscles. She curled her legs up against him. "I feel a little scared."

"Of what?"

"I don't know. Like everything about this is too perfect." Instantly she remembered the deadly growth consuming her, and stopped caressing him. "I'm cold," and she pulled the blanket up around her.

"No one has ever touched me like you do."

"I like touching you. I could touch you for hours, days."

He kissed her sweetly. "We fit together so nicely, too. Have you noticed?"

"Um, hm."

"You know, I wanted to make love to you since the first moment I met you at Opeakaa Falls."

She nestled closer to him, snuggling into his arms. "Me, too. You know, I've never had an orgasm making love the first time."

"That's good," he said so quietly she almost couldn't hear him.

"I feel like we've been practicing making love for a long time."

Lani didn't reply. His eyes were closed and his breathing was deep and regular. After a few minutes he mumbled something incoherent.

"What did you say?"

His body jerked. "What?" He yawned again. "I'm falling asleep."

But Sarah could have sworn she heard him say in a whisper, "I love you," and she fell asleep thinking of those words.

Hours later she woke with a start. The bed was empty next to her, and she could hear faint movement in the room. "Lani?"

"I'm right here," he said in the dark.

"Where are you going?"

"I need to drive home and get my stuff ready. I have to catch a plane from Lihue at six."

"Oh," she said, sleepily, yawning and stretching. "What time is it?"

"About two. Go back to sleep."

"When will I see you?"

"Later today or tomorrow. I'll call you when I get back.""

"Okay," she agreed, turning on her side, and soon was breathing heavily.

After he had finished dressing, he leaned over and kissed the sleeping woman on the cheek, then slipped quietly out of the hotel room, closing the door gently behind him.

Chapter 5

Mahina's Tale Continues

I stubbornly refused to believe my husband was dead. I prayed that he was only lost and would eventually find his way back to me. I walked that beach many days and nights, calling to him until I was hoarse. Waiting in the darkness of our hut, my eyes bloodshot from crying. But time went by and he never returned.

Periodically my father came to check on me and bring me food.

"My daughter," he said to me one day, "you must eat. Your cheeks are getting hollow," sitting next to me on the sand. He put his arm around me and I wearily leaned against him, snuggling against the refuge of his bare shoulder.

I looked up at his craggy face. "But I am not hungry, Papa," I told him. "My stomach bothers me all the time and I cannot keep my food down."

"I worry about you. You are so thin; you are beginning to look like a spirit instead of a woman." He patted my head lovingly.

I could only shrug, sifting through the sand aimlessly with my fingers, staring at the horizon, waiting and wishing.

"Come back and live with your mother and me. We will take care of you."

I reluctantly nodded in agreement and he helped me moved my few possessions to my family home.

After a while, my rebellious stomach settled down. My mother was the first to realize that I was putting on weight. She touched my bloated abdomen. "Do you still get your moon times?"

I thought about her question for a few moments. "No, not since…" I didn't finish my sentence.

She knew what I meant, but didn't press me. "How about your breasts?"

"What about my breasts?"

"Do they hurt?"

"Yes, they have been very sore lately."

She touched one gently, and I grimaced.

"I think you will have a baby." She sounded excited.

"A baby?" I was stunned by the news. I knew I had no love left in me for a baby or anyone else. My heart was dry and empty, like the desert side of our island. I turned away so she could not see the misery in my eyes.

"We must tell his family right away."

"Why?" I muttered.

"So that they can arrange for you and the baby to be taken care of." A husband's family often provided for widows and their children.

My mother hurried away to talk to them. Sometime later I was formally introduced to my husband's oldest brother, who had no wife. I recognized him easily by the crimson, jagged scar that ran down the entire left side of his face. He had been attacked by a wild pig in his boyhood days of hunting and had been permanently disfigured.

He sat with me in the early evening on a mat outside his hut, while our two families discussed the details of our marriage. His manner was quite reserved, as he tried to work up courage to confront me.

"Do you find me repulsive?" he finally asked bluntly.

"No, not especially," I lied.

"You would be the first woman who did not," he replied bitterly. "If only you could overlook my appearance and see the love I have for you inside me."

I felt pity for the man and touched his scar gently.

He pulled away. "If you do not wish to marry me, let me know now."

"I do wish to marry you." The words echoed hollowly inside my head.

My brother-in-law examined my face for a long time until he felt confident that I spoke the truth. His body seemed to grow taller with my reply. "Do you know I have loved you for a long time?"

"No, I never knew that." I felt sick hearing his words. *Who was he talking about? It couldn't be me. He loved the carefree, happy young girl I once was but would never be again.* I thought these things in wild despair.

"I always envied my brother," he continued with his confession. "But of course I could never compete with him," and he touched his cheek. "Now I get what I have wished for all along, to have you for myself."

My chest ached terribly at the mention of my dead husband and I put my hand on the pain.

"I am sorry I mentioned him," he apologized.

"It is nothing." But the pain spread throughout my chest, a constricting wound that would never heal. "We both have scars," I murmured. "Mine is inside."

He put his arms tightly around me, but they were cold, chilled from the evening air. I felt smothered with the urgency of his embrace, but I did not move or protest.

My parents arranged for us to marry quickly, before my dead husband's baby could be born.

There was another village wedding, but the bride didn't smile, and the villagers didn't seem as cheerful as the last one they had attended. My mother made another lei, this time out of local pink orchids. And then I moved into the newly constructed hut with my brother-in-law husband.

We made awkward love on our wedding night, as our arms and legs became tangled; our bodies were strangers to each other.

"Did I hurt you?" he asked anxiously.

"No. You were fine," I reassured him, and turned on my side, trying to hold back the flood of grief.

"I am very sorry," he added, and put his arm around my waist in a protective gesture.

But from that moment on, I would allow no further intimacy between us. I understand now that I was young and selfish, clinging to my old love as a child clings to its mother. But I was unable to open myself up to him. My new husband was good to me, though, and very patient; however, my crowded memories allowed no others into my heart.

"Have you learned to care for me yet?" he asked me often, with an insistent tone of voice, as though I might change my mind.

I always replied in the same petulant way. "I will never let myself love ever again."

Although he turned away to hide his expression, his face flushed with anger and resentment.

I performed my household chores as though I was asleep. Cooked the taro. Mashed it into poi. Cleaned and cooked the fish my husband caught for our meals. Brushed the sand off our sleeping mats. Often I would sit on the beach for hours, staring at the waves beyond the coral reef, until the sky began to turn pink with the hues of sunset.

My back ached relentlessly. Sometimes I could sense the little one inside me move, but I felt no joy. I only felt very, very tired, older than the wrinkled, toothless crones of the village. Life seemed to be one endless day, followed by one sleepless night, after another.

When my husband turned in his sleep and put his arm over me, I carefully pushed it off, trying not to wake him. If he tried to hug me, I would shy away. I could see unhappiness in his drooping shoulders, but his melancholy was no more than mine.

When my labor pains began, he hurried to bring the midwives to help me. I felt detached from my body, from the events occurring to me, as though the birth process belonged to someone else. I screamed with each contraction, yet my voice sounded disembodied. Hours later the son of my dead husband was born, but I felt no pleasure. As though from a great distance, I could hear the child's squalling.

One of the midwives wrapped him in a new tapa cloth, handed the child to my mother, who brought him to me.

I put my arm over my eyes.

"It is time for you to nurse your son," she pressured me.

"Take him away," I replied in a muffled voice. My breasts were empty and lifeless.

Suddenly I felt wetness gush from between my legs.

"Somebody help her!" my mother screamed, noticing the red torrent.

I became aware of frantic movement around me, as the women tried to stop my bleeding. I floated out of my body, watching as several of the midwives tried to staunch the flow, their hands and arms drenched scarlet.

My mother watched, horrified, as my body grew pale and limp. "Do something! Please, help my daughter!" Her anguished cries grew louder as the sand under my body became stained with my life's blood.

After some time, one of the women went outside to find my husband, to tell him the news. "Your wife is dead, but you have a healthy son."

My mother began to wail in lament.

I felt weightless and free, and began to float above the scene, beyond the hut I had shared with a man I didn't love. I drifted serenely above the white, fluffy clouds surrounding our island home into the masses of stars beyond the sky. Then I soared down a long, dark tunnel. At its end I could see a brilliant glow. I hoped my beloved was there. "Wait for me, my love!" I cried but no answer was forthcoming. My husband's spirit had already departed the spirit world, in a hurry to be born again into another body, to be close to me once again. He was the child I left behind, now left in the care of his scarred brother.

Chapter 6

Jim Diamond

When Sarah woke up, her head was aching with intense pressure. She sat up, swung her legs out of bed, and felt a rush of vertigo. "Oh," she moaned, trying to orient herself. The room was swirling in circles. Closing her eyes, she willed herself steady. As she gazed around the room again, the dizziness passed. However, she realized that her vision was blurry and she was seeing two of everything again.

She stumbled to the bathroom, bumping into the wall along the way, feeling the rest of her way with her hands. She looked in the mirror but all she saw looking back at her was two images of herself and both of those were clouded. Dr. Eberhardt's words came to mind: "The tumor is pressing on the optic nerve." She sighed. "No wonder I'm having trouble seeing." She squinted at herself, but the reflection didn't get any clearer. In the mirror were hazy blotches of color, reflecting the flowery wallpaper as well as her coppery red hair. Near the base of her skull, she could feel tendrils of pain reaching into her head.

Sarah put her hand to her throbbing head, as the inescapable reality of her deadly situation descended like a black haze on her thoughts. "Maybe I should have listened to Dr. Eberhardt." But stubbornly, she forced herself to focus on the current situation instead.

"There must be other ways to cure this thing." She vaguely remembered a book. "Norman somebody," she tried to recollect, tapping her chin with her finger. "Cousins. That's it. Norman Cousins. He cured his cancer by watching comedies and taking vitamin C." She pointed at the still-indistinct vision in front of her. "If he could do it, why can't I?"

She made a decision. "I'm going to the nearest library and bookstore, and read every book that has ever come out about healing cancer." She grimaced at the "C" word. "I don't need to take this verdict this lying down." She shrugged stubbornly and the woman in front of her shrugged simultaneously. "And I don't have to do what doctors tell me. The methods seem barbaric to me. They're still practicing." She smiled grimly. "This is my body and I'm going to...uh, do...something different."

She eased her way back into the bedroom. "I'm glad Lani's not here. He'd just worry about me," she thought to herself. She sat down on the bed. "I miss him already." She tried to look at her wristwatch without much success. "He's only been gone a few hours," she guessed. Her heart lurched, thinking of the tall Hawaiian whom she gotten close to in two days.

"Maybe I'm crazy, getting involved too fast. I hardly know him. Besides, there's the..." She stopped herself, again not wanting to admit the ominous possibilities that lay ahead. She felt around for the phone. "Room service? Could you send up some orange juice, fresh papaya." She thought quickly. "And a couple of poached eggs with toast. Make that dry, whole wheat toast." She remembered researching articles on nutrition.

Then she felt her way into the bathroom and took a long hot bath, luxuriating in the water, sliding down until most of her body was submerged. Periodically she would add more hot water and tried to forget in the soothing warmth.

She had just gotten out of the tub, put on a long cotton shift and was drying her hair, when she heard a knock at the door. "Lani?" she thought as she hurried to open it, even though he had told her he would be in Honolulu that day. "Maybe…"

"Room service."

"Oh, yeah," she replied, with a disappointed twinge. She indicated the table near the windows, and the young man set it down. She gave him a tip for delivering it. He was a blend of Polynesian, Asian, and some Filipino, and reminded her of Lani, although they looked nothing alike. "Thanks," she smiled.

"Thank you, ma'am," and he closed the door lightly.

"Ma'am." That's what Lani had called her humorously the first day they met. "But ma'am is what you call an older woman." She made a face and anxiously felt around her mouth and eyes for evidence of wrinkles. "Ma'am."

As she sat down to eat, Sarah noticed that the blurred vision had cleared somewhat, but she was still seeing double, which made her lightheaded.

So many thoughts swirled through her mind, that she had a hard time tasting her food. Thoughts of Lani. The consequences of leaving L.A. and her career. Images of her illness. She bit down hard on the dry toast, angry at herself. "How did this happen? Am I a bad person? Is God punishing me?" Intellectually, she knew that people who acquire a terrible disease asked these kinds of questions. She'd interviewed more than a few. But knowing that didn't help now. She wanted Lani to be there, to hold her in his muscular arms, to tell her everything was going to be all right, to kiss her. She began to feel tingly, thinking about him, wanting him. "Sarah Arlington," she reprimanded herself out loud, "get a grip."

After breakfast, she laid down on the bed, praying that her eyesight would improve, but the double vision continued along with the woozy feeling. She tried to remember everything she had ever heard or read about natural healing. "Maybe I should have gone to Lourdes instead," she complained.

She fumed impatiently, tossing and turning on the bed, restless to take some action, any action. Then she got a notebook out of her suitcase, fumbled for a pen out of her purse, and began to write some notations in very big, awkward letters.

"Healthy diet. Physical therapies. Meditation. Psychic healers." At the last entry, she looked out the window, trying to focus on the coconut palm outside. "Yeah. Right." She crossed out "psychic healers." "How am I going to research about what to do if I can't even see?" she asked herself, suddenly aware of her situation. "I don't think I have enough time to learn Braille. Just kidding," she reminded herself. She threw the pen across the room in a sudden burst of anger. "Damn it!" she exclaimed. "What am I going to do?"

Sarah could feel tears smarting at her eyes, and wiped them away with the back of her hand. "I need a plan. Not self-pity." But she was overwhelmed by the turmoil of emotions emerging from within. "Maybe I shouldn't have come here. Maybe I should have listened to Dr. Eberhardt, and gotten radiated. Maybe I shouldn't have let Lani get so close. It's not fair to him. He doesn't know what he's gotten into." Despite all her efforts, suppressing her emotions failed and a torrent of confusion, sadness, and fear streaked down her cheeks.

She cried for a while, thinking of the most terrible things she could think of, submerging herself in worst-case scenarios.

"When Lani comes back, I'll be completely blind, and then he'll leave me. When that happens, I'll die in the hotel, with only room service for comfort." She cried harder, drowning in a sea of hopelessness and despair. "For heaven's sakes, Sarah. Don't have a Pity Party," she admonished herself.

She got up and started pacing the room, lurching about in an uncoordinated manner, tears still streaming down her face. "What has my life been about? Have I made any difference? Will my dying affect anything or anyone?" She teetered a little, as a wave of vertigo washed over her, and she sat down again.

"I don't know what to do. Who can help me? I should have kept in touch with people. Now I have no one. I want Lani, but he's at his conference, dammit. What should I do? Why did I ever come here?"

But there were no answers to any of her questions.

Slowly, the emotional storm passed. Sarah stumbled into the bathroom and washed her face, feeling emotionally purged and calmer.

"I can see better, too" she realized. As she glanced out the window, the palm tree looked more well-defined. As she got dressed, she started humming "Bali Hai" again. Putting her eye make-up on was difficult, so she only used some blush and lipstick. Then she picked up the pen she had thrown against the wall, put it back in her purse, took her notebook, and locked up the room. At the lobby, she paused momentarily to ask directions. Then she got into her rental car and drove to the local library.

Sarah browsed through the computerized directory of the library, picking out more than a dozen books on alternative health care, cancer, and other associated topics. She had done this kind of investigation many times before, using a shotgun approach when researching a subject she was going to write about. But never before had the study been so intensely personal. She got out her laptop, and made notes, skimming the books in front of her, squinting as she did so.

Her stomach began rumbling loudly and Sarah felt empty. She looked at the wall clock. "Five o'clock." She rubbed her neck and stretched. "I've been at this for six hours." Her laptop was full of notes, and she hadn't even looked through all the books she had stacked up. "Some of these are kind of old already," she noticed. "Guess I should try the internet next." Her stomach growled again. "The next vital question is —where am I going to eat?"

When she went to find her rental car, a breeze had picked up but the air was still warm, even though the sun was getting low in the sky. "I think I'd like to have dinner on the beach." She asked the librarian if there were any hotels or resorts facing the water, and was directed to a large resort in Kapaa, minutes away from the library.

Sarah leaned back in the ample chair, at a table facing the ocean, and sipped a Mai Tai. Ordinarily she didn't enjoy tropical drinks, but here they tasted delicious. She ordered some local fresh ahi for dinner and realized how hungry she had gotten. She flipped open her laptop, forming correlations and conclusions. Sarah Arlington had an uncanny ability to put aside her own concerns when she was exploring information. She got so involved, she didn't notice an exceptionally tanned, good-looking blonde man staring at her from across the veranda.

The waiter came by with another drink.

"I didn't order this."

"The man over there sent it to you," and he pointed to the debonair man, who waved at her and smiled.

Sarah nodded slightly, then returned to her notes, crossing some things out, and circling other notations.

The blonde-haired man sauntered up to her table, his own drink in hand.

"I hope you don't mind my curiosity, but I was wondering what an attractive woman like you is doing working on such a glorious evening?" He smiled a toothy smile.

"Hmmm?" she replied, and looked up at him.

He was wearing expensive gray slacks and a black shirt, with purple and yellow flowers. "Jim Diamond," he boomed, holding out his hand.

She noticed a gold ring mounted with an ostentatious diamond on his right pinkie finger. Sarah glanced at his proffered hand, feeling a little annoyed at being interrupted. She quickly squeezed his hand, and noticed it was clammy. "Sarah Arlington," she said, and looked at the screen, hoping he'd go away.

But instead Jim pulled out a chair and boldly sat down. "What's that you're doing?" he asked, inquisitively.

She hastily closed the laptop. "I'm reviewing notes for a story I'm doing," she lied.

"Are you a writer?"

"Journalist."

"Who do you work for?"

"I'm freelance right now."

"What's the story on?"

"You ask more questions than a reporter," she retorted. When he didn't reply, she added, "Alternative health care."

"That's a great subject."

"Yeah," she agreed.

"Where are you staying?"

"Why are you asking me all these questions?" she asked in an aggravated tone of voice.

"I'm not prying. Just trying to get a conversation started." He smiled affably, at ease with himself.

Sarah felt contrite. "I'm sorry. I guess I'm not a very good conversationalist right now."

"A lot of things on your mind?"

She nodded. "A lot of things." She swallowed the last of her Mai Tai.

"Can I buy you another?"

"Why not? They're addicting."

Jim waved the waitress over and ordered another round. "So how long are you visiting the island?"

"I'm not sure."

"Are you here with anyone?"

"Not exactly." All of a sudden Sarah felt lonely, thinking of Lani.

The fair-haired man beamed when he heard her answer and pulled his chair a little closer. "Are you staying at this hotel?"

"No, in Poipu."

"Not very far from here."

"No," she agreed.

"Have any plans for this evening?"

Sarah thought of the books she had scanned and the millions of internet sites waiting to be googled, then felt an overwhelming weariness. "I was going to do some more research." Sadness blew over her like the wind through the nearby palms.

He saw the shift in her attitude, and immediately felt solicitous. He tentatively touched her hand. "You look like you're carrying the weight of the world." When she didn't reply, Jim changed the subject. "I'm a musician. I sing and play the piano at the cocktail lounge here. But I'm not scheduled to go on until 9:00." He paused.

Sarah was looking out at the ocean, not paying attention. *What would Lani do if he knew I had cancer?* she thought about the Polynesian man. *Leave me, probably. I should end our affair before I'm too involved — and get hurt.*

"So we have lots of time. We can fling off our clothes and run naked on the beach." He laughed.

"Hmmm? I'm sorry. What were you saying?"

"That's okay. It's not important. Just trying to get your attention."

The cocktail waitress returned with their drinks.

"To your health," he said, raising his glass.

"I'll drink to that," she assented heartily.

"You know, you're very beautiful."

"Thanks." She could feel the headache starting again, deep inside her head, making her eyes burn.

"I'd like to spend some time getting to know you."

Jim's face was very close, and Sarah could detect a tiny spark of sincerity in his eyes. An inexpressible longing for safety, for security overwhelmed her. *A bird in the hand...* she mused. Just then the waiter brought her dinner and she didn't reply.

Sarah ate while Jim chatted. "Aren't you going to eat?" she finally asked him.

"No, I usually have a late dinner, after my show."

"Mmmm," was her reply, while chewing a mouthful of food.

"But I'll have one of your rolls."

"Help yourself."

He hunted around for another topic, since the lovely woman wasn't paying much attention. He felt uncomfortable, but persisted. "Your eyes are an interesting color. In this light I can't tell if they're blue or green."

"Actually, they're kind of a blue-green." She studied his intense blue eyes. His blonde hair was streaked by the sun, which was neatly combed back and sprayed stiffly into place. "Have you always lived here?" she asked.

"I visited Kauai with my parents in the 60s. I am, or was, an avid surfer and couldn't get enough. So after I graduated high school, I moved here."

"But I thought you said you're a professional pianist."

"I've always had talent. My parents hoped I'd eventually go to Julliard, then become a concert pianist. They're disappointed that I've settled for playing in bars and such. I'm getting a little old for surfing anyway."

Sarah examined Jim's face. "How old are you?" she asked bluntly.

"Forty-five."

"You look younger."

"Thanks, I can use a well-placed compliment. Why do you ask?"

She smiled. "I wanted to know how old you consider old."

"You're even more beautiful when you smile."

She grimaced at his banal compliments. Her dinner finished, the busboy came to remove her dishes. She ordered rich Kona coffee and macadamia nut ice cream for dessert. "Are you sure you wouldn't like something?" Sarah asked Jim.

"No, I'm fine. I had a snack before I came out here." He gulped down the rest of his cocktail, and ordered another. He noticed her glance. "Another talent of mine, which comes in handy where I work. I can drink all night and not get drunk."

"A dubious accomplishment," she said ironically. She was feeling woozy and had indigestion. She rubbed her abdomen. "Too much rich food."

"You know, we seem to have gotten off on the wrong foot. Maybe I should go out and come back. Start all over again." He held out his hand as a joke. "Hi. My name is Jim Diamond and…"

"No, it's just me," she interrupted. "I haven't been feeling well lately."

"Sorry to hear that. Nothing serious, I hope?" The worried look on his ruddy face, burned by many days in the sun, seemed genuine.

Sarah hesitated, and he interrupted her.

"Have you ever been to Hawaii before?"

She was grateful for his questions now, giving her a chance to small talk. "I came here to cover a story about a hurricane and fell in love with Kauai. Just like you did," she realized suddenly. "I guess we have that in common."

"We sure do."

She gagged and burped up a vile taste in her mouth. Then she felt an ominous gurgling in her stomach. "Oh, oh," she said. "Excuse me," and she ran to the ladies room. When she got there, she vomited violently over and over until her stomach was empty.

"Are you okay in there?" Jim's voice echoed through the closed door.

"I'll be right out." She went to the basin, and washed up. She looked at her reflection. Her face was pasty white, while her cheeks and neck were bright red. Her hair looked disheveled. She went to the door of the restroom and opened it.

"Geez, you look awful," he said.

She gave him an annoyed look. "Thanks."

"What's the matter?"

"I have cancer," she said curtly, deliberately dropping the emotional bombshell on the piano player, hoping to get rid of him.

"Oh, my god!" he spluttered. His concern was replaced by agitation. He looked around anxiously, trying to find appropriate words to say.

"The tumor's in my brain." Sarah wrinkled up her forehead.

Jim's face was a portrait of turmoil. "I can't tell you how sorry I am. Geez. I've been talking up a storm, while you...You must think I'm totally insensitive."

But Sarah didn't. "No," she said, touching his hand firmly. "Actually I'm relieved to finally talk about it with somebody." She breathed a deep sigh and let it out audibly.

"Are these side effects from chemotherapy?"

"No, from the tumor pressing on my brain. I've been getting headaches, dizziness, blurred vision. Nausea is a new one." She chuckled humorlessly.

"You sure it wasn't dinner?"

"No, I don't think so. The symptoms are getting worse, especially at night."

"Let me take you to the emergency room."

"No, I'd rather not. Besides you have to go to work in a while. Emergency rooms take hours." She was starting to sway ominously.

"That's true," he admitted. "But you're looking awfully pale. Where are you staying?"

"The Poipu Sheraton."

"I know where it is. I played there two years ago. But it's almost half an hour away and you're in no condition to drive. My place is just a few minutes from here. How about I take you there and you can rest?"

"I couldn't ask you to do that. I feel embarrassed enough as it is."

"You're not asking. I'm offering."

"Maybe I should. I'm really dizzy and weak."

"You see, you shouldn't be driving."

"Thanks," she agreed reluctantly.

He handed over her belongings.

"Oh, my gosh, I forgot all about my stuff."

"I know. Also I persuaded the management to write off your dinner bill. I told them you were in here throwing it up." He grinned.

"Thanks so much," and she paused, chagrined. "I forgot your name."

"Jim."

"Jim. You're a saint."

"Saint Jim, that's me. Protector of sick women." He smiled grimly and held out his hand. Sarah took it tentatively, still unsteady on her feet.

Chapter 7

Dr. Namagushi

Jim drove her up the hill to his home. "When I found out about my cancer, I decided to sell all my stuff and move to Kauai. It seemed like a good idea at the time," she said, continuing their conversation.

"But now?"

"I'm not sure anymore." She shrugged her shoulders, looking suddenly like a small, helpless child. "I'm a stranger in a strange land"

"Robert Heinlein."

"Right." She nodded. "I read that book years ago. Somehow I understand it now."

"Must be tough," he added.

Jim drove up into his driveway. Hibiscus plants were had been planted neatly around the property, now blooming in glorious red, yellow, and orange hues. A banana tree vigorously grew in the corner, next to the freshly painted house. The grass had been recently mowed. He got out and opened the front door for Sarah.

Sarah looked around with curiosity. Jim's house was immaculately clean and looked newly decorated. The furniture was light-colored wood furniture, with glass-topped tables constructed out of cane.

"How long have you lived here?" she asked him when he returned.

"About two years. Do you like it?"

"It's quite attractive, but looks like you just moved in."

He laughed. "People say that all the time."

"You're awfully tidy for a man."

"That's because I'm a Virgo. Virgos are known to be well-organized and clean."

"I'm afraid to touch anything or sit down."

"Go ahead. I have a housekeeper that comes in once a week."

"Must be nice," she said, gingerly sitting down on a white couch, with floral and white cushions carefully arranged. "I like having a clean house, but I'd rather have fun than clean. I should've hired someone years ago."

Jim had a sudden brainstorm and sat down next to her. "Why don't you check out of your hotel and stay here instead? I have plenty of room, two bedrooms, two baths. We wouldn't get in each other's way. And I could take care of you."

"Good heavens, no!" she exclaimed. "I didn't tell you about my problem to make you feel sorry for me."

"I know, but I'd like to have you here just the same."

"I'll think about it."

"You can trust me. I'm not a serial killer or anything like that."

She laughed nervously. "I didn't think you were." She considered for a few moments, while he held his breath. Fear clenched her stomach and she saw Lani's face. "No thank you, It's not a good idea. You'd be responsible for me if, or when, anything happened. That's asking a lot.

You don't even know me."

"I want to. That's what I'm trying to tell you. I don't know how good a nurse I'd be, but I'm willing to find out."

"No," she said firmly.

"Okay," he agreed. "But you'll let me help out when I can, won't you?"

"Are you always this impulsive?" She looked at her watch. "You've only known me two hours."

"I follow my gut instincts."

"Well, I don't!" she snapped, then thought quickly of Lani and a stain of mortification colored her pale, wan face.

"I've got to be leaving for work soon. Why don't you take a shower and freshen up while I'm gone?"

"I will. Thank you again for today. You're really amazing."

"Don't mention it. Um, by the way, shouldn't you call your doctor or something?"

"I don't have one."

"You're kidding."

"No," she replied slowly.

"Then tomorrow I'm going to take you to see my doctor."

"I'd rather not," she replied stubbornly.

"Listen, Sarah, you should take better care of yourself." He sounded adamant.

"Okay, okay," she relented.

"And you'll need someone to help you."

"I've always been extremely self-sufficient. I'm not used to the idea of someone rescuing me. I don't like it," and she wrinkled up her nose.

"Don't think of it as rescuing. Think of it more like helping a friend."

"I guess you're right," but she sounded unconvinced.

"How did you…uh,…I mean, what are you doing for your symptoms?"

"The doctor wanted me to start radiation, but I didn't like the idea of having my hair fall out." She bit her lip. "Sounds like a lame excuse, doesn't it?" When he didn't reply, she continued. "I was at the library today to research how other people cured themselves." She looked pensive. "So far no one mentioned curing brain cancer." Then she brightened momentarily. "But I could be the first."

"You're not doing anything then?"

"Nope. Just muddling through."

"Do you have any pain medication?"

"I didn't think of it until recently."

Jim rolled his eyes in exasperation. "Well, it's getting late. I better get going. Just make yourself at home and rest—while you're here, that is." And he left for work.

She washed up. Then she looked around the house and found what seemed the smaller of the two bedrooms, assuming it was for guests. Sarah pulled off her clothes, got in between the sheets, drawing the elegant comforter up around her neck, as she looked around the room decorated in modern Polynesian decor. There were no personal touches, such as photographs, and the room was very tidy. *Everything about Jim is orderly,* she thought. *Unusual for a man.*

She hoped the pressure of the pillow underneath would help the pain in her head that seemed to come and go, like waves on the beach. Fortunately, her nausea had subsided. But the dizziness increased in that position, and she rolled over on her side. She thought of the tall Hawaiian and wondered if Lani had returned from his conference, but she didn't have his phone number. "I could call the hotel, and see if he left a message," she thought. But she was too drained to take any action. She clicked off the light on the nightstand. The sun had set and Sarah felt lonely and anxious in the darkening room. "I guess I shouldn't have taken Jim up on his offer. But what else could I do?" She fretted for a bit until she drifted off to sleep.

Meanwhile the conference had run late and Lani had missed his flight back to Kauai, so he checked into the hotel hosting the conference. He couldn't get to sleep, but kept tossing and turning, ruminating about the tall, beautiful redhead that had captured his attention and roused his inmost feelings. He clicked on the light, got out his cellphone, and searched information for Sarah's hotel in Poipu. "I hope I'm not calling too late," as he selected the number for her hotel. But more than anything, he wanted to hear her voice. Just as two days had seemed too short to create such a profound connection, so the day he had spent away from her seemed endless and unbearable.

"I'm sorry. Miss Arlington's room doesn't answer. Would you care to leave a message?" asked a polite desk clerk.

He looked at his watch. 2:20 am. "Where could she be?" An ominous feeling started to percolate in the pit of his stomach. "No. No message," and he slammed the phone down. His face reddened from humiliation and jealousy. "Where is she? Why isn't she there? Where could she be at this hour?" He tried to lie down again, but he was too restless. Lani got up and paced the small room. Black thoughts swirled through his mind. *I should listen to myself more often. You just can't trust women, Lani. The moment you turn your back, they're fooling around with somebody else.* He looked at his watch again. 2:30. *I knew it was too good to be true. She's just another haole woman wanting to have a fling with a local, pretending for a few weeks that she's a native!* With that, he threw back the cover on the bed and lay down. But sleep would elude him.

While Lani raged, Sarah was dreaming she was on a brilliant beach. In the distance was a stand of palm trees. There was a small, dilapidated hut on the beach a few feet from her. Some of the palm fronds had fallen away. She walked over to the hut and peered in. It was dim inside and she couldn't see very well. A pallet that looked like a bed lay on the floor, and some tapa cloth hung on the wall. As she looked around at the disarray, a sense of loneliness and despair pervaded the dream. She heard a noise and turned around, expecting to see Lani. But instead she saw Jim. He smiled and took her resolutely by the hand.

Sarah followed wordlessly.

He led her to another hut, larger and intact. He stepped aside to let her enter. Inside the hut was death, waiting for her. She turned to say something to Jim, but he had gone. A stranger stood in the doorway. He had on a necklace with a very large shark's tooth hanging from it. In her nightmare she screamed when she saw his frightfully scarred face. "Lani!" she cried. "Lani, where are you?"

"Lani," moaned Sarah, softly, awake now, but still frightened. It took her a few moments to realize that she had been dreaming. Then she got up and fumbled around, looking for a light switch. She finally found one in the bedroom and eased her way into the adjoining bathroom, which was decorated with brown-and-white tiles on the floor and up the walls and had sparkling golden fixtures on the sink. "One thing I'll say for Mr. Diamond. He's got excellent taste." The bathroom sink, tile and toilet gleamed. Sarah splashed warm water on her face and turned out the light.

Then she returned and fell onto the bed. "I shouldn't be here," she murmured to herself, but realized she couldn't leave. She had left her rental car in the hotel parking lot. "Something is terribly wrong. I wish I could figure out what it is."

She got out her cell phone. She found the number for her hotel, and dialed the front desk of the Sheraton. "This is Sarah Hamilton, room 1211. Do I have any messages? No? Thank you," and she hung up. The effort made her fatigued and dizzy again, and she lay down and fell into a troubled sleep.

A pink sunrise was tinting the windows of Jim's house, when Sarah woke up again. The blonde, tanned man lay next to her, face up, under the sheet. The sheet barely covered his curly brown hair on his chest. She realized in a second that Jim was lying naked in bed next to her. She jumped up, but felt an immediate rush of nausea and vertigo and sat down just as quickly.

Jim stirred. He put his hand out next to him and found only empty space. Then he opened his eyes, which were streaked with red, looking for Sarah. "Good morning, sweetheart."

She grimaced at the word. "How long have you been there?" She could barely contain her outrage.

"Since about three. You were sleeping soundly and I didn't want to wake you."

Sarah felt a torrent of emotions, anger and guilt mostly. "I wish you had." She was pulling on her clothes. "Why didn't you sleep in your own bed?"

"I wanted to be with you."

"Please take me home. Back to the hotel, I mean," she added.

"Give me a few more hours sleep," he asked drowsily.

"I'd like to go home—now," she insisted.

"All right. I'm getting up," and he shuffled into the bathroom, eyes barely open. "Jeez, it's only 6:30." Then he sleepily walked into the kitchen.

She could hear him opening and closing cupboards. "What are you doing?" she called.

"Making coffee. I'm no good without a couple of cups in the morning. Want some?"

"No. Thank you." She sat on the edge of the bed, fuming.

After a few minutes, he came back into the bedroom. He was still naked.

"Do you think you can put something on?" she said angrily, averting her eyes.

"Oh, sure," and he slipped on his briefs. "How are you feeling this morning?"

"Better, but not great," she replied, tersely.

"Hey, what's the matter?"

"I thought you were going to drive me home last night."

"Wouldn't make a lot of sense. I'd have to wake you up, take you to your hotel. Then drive back here. Get a few hours sleep. Then drive back to your hotel, pick you up and take you to the doctor." He paused for emphasis.

She was nodding. "Yeah. I understand what you're saying."

"But you're still not happy?"

"No," she replied emphatically.

He went to his closet in the next room and selected a clean shirt and a freshly pressed pair of slacks to wear. Then he got out his cellphone and dialed.

Sarah could overhear his conversation.

"Hello, Hiro? Jim Diamond. Yeah. How're ya doing, doc?" He listened for a moment. "Fine," he answered. "Listen, I have a big favor. There's a girl I know, needs to be seen—right away."

Sarah was already dressed and went in to wash up and brush her hair, still eavesdropping.

"Yeah, I know. Last minute. But this is really urgent, you know?" He listened again. "No, no. Nothing like that. This girl is really sick. Cancer she tells me. She's throwing up, has terrible headaches, and can't see real well either."

The doctor apparently spoke, while Jim listened. "I know. I'm just that kind of guy," and he laughed. "Okay. Thanks, Hiro. We'll be there at eight. Yeah, you, too."

She came out and sat down on the unmade bed.

"We're all set. He can see you at eight, before his regular appointments."

"How did you do it?"

"He owes me," he replied without further explanation.

"Why don't you drive me back to my hotel. I'll get my car and drive there myself. You won't have to bother."

"It's no bother. How's your vision?"

"A little dizzy. That's all."

He studied her for a moment. "I'm not letting you drive." Then he went into the kitchen, coming back with a steaming mug of coffee. He sat it down carefully on the nightstand, after taking a few swallows. Then he wordlessly went in to take a shower.

Sarah proceeded into the kitchen to find something to eat. She found some bananas in a bowl, and slowly ate one, sitting down on a high stool at the kitchen counter. By now the sun had fully risen, and Sarah could feel the warmth radiating through the glass windows. She could hear the sound of the blowdryer from the bathroom. She was thirsty and looked through the cabinets to find a glass. To her amazement, all the glasses were lined up perfectly by size. "It figures," she mentioned to herself, selected a glass and drew some water from the sink.

Shortly after, Jim came out, fully dressed and carrying his empty mug. She noticed he was wearing shoes with socks. Her heart skipped a beat.

He filled his cup from the coffee maker again. "Can I fix you something to eat?"

"No, thank you," she answered more politely, having relaxed a little. "I had a banana and now my stomach feels better."

He got out a bowl and some granola and milk and sat down to eat.

"How about the rest of you?"

"I'm okay." She swallowed, trying to ignore the bad taste in her mouth. "I feel like I was a big baby yesterday."

"Hey, cut it out" he said. "You'd do the same for me, wouldn't you?" He smiled warmly.

Sarah silently admitted to herself that she probably wouldn't. Not that she was an uncaring person, but the situation was extremely peculiar, and there was something odd about Jim. "I don't know," was all she said.

When he finished, he rinsed off all the dishes, put them in the dishwasher, put the milk and granola away, and cleaned off the counter.

She went into the bedroom to retrieve her purse and noticed Jim had made the bed as good as any hotel maid.

As the handsome man drove her to the doctor's, Sarah tried to evaluate the last few days. But the jumble of her thoughts was matched by the whirling of emotions.

When they got to Dr. Namagushi's office, she was feeling headachy. Jim's friend was waiting for them.

"Hey, buddy." Hiro Namagushi shook hands with Jim Diamond. "Aloha," he said, turning to her.

"Sarah Arlington," and she shook his hand.

He punched his friend's arm. "You didn't tell me she was beautiful." Jim smiled possessively.

"Come on in," and he beckoned them into his private office. When Sarah and Jim had settled into leather armchairs, the internist came right to the point. "Jim tells me you have been diagnosed with brain cancer?"

"Yes, that's right."

"And lately you're having some visual problems, nausea, headaches. That kind of thing."

"Right again."

"Did your doctor mention where the tumor was, what kind and size?"

"He said it was very large and was pressing on the optical nerve."

"What kind of treatment have you had for this?"

"He said he couldn't operate. And I haven't done anything else."

"What?" The physician leaned forward in his chair, astounded. "No radiation either?"

"Mmmm, mmmm," was her sheepish reply.

The doctor scratched his head, ruffling his coarse Asian hair until some of it stood straight up, making the doctor look slightly silly.

Sarah muffled a childish desire to giggle.

"When were you diagnosed?"

"Let's see." She squinted her eyes, trying to focus her unruly brain. "About eleven, twelve, maybe fourteen days ago."

"What kind of testing did they do?"

"X-rays. MRI. CT scan. Probed around with some needles, too."

"Hmmmm." The Asian man leaned back in his swivel chair.

Sarah looked at Jim, who was watching his friend's worried expression.

"Did he explain to you that without radiation, the tumor could create all kinds of other problems?"

"Yes, but I didn't think…"

He interrupted her. "Your headaches. Are they getting worse?"

"Yes, much worse."

"And are you having dizzy spells, blurred or double vision, nausea, vomiting."

"Yes, but…"

"Sarah, I'm going to tell you straight. I'm not an oncologist, but I do know something about cancer. You're in big trouble, unless you get radiation right away, to shrink the tumor. Otherwise…" He left the rest unsaid.

Sarah felt prickles of fear down her spine.

"These symptoms are letting you know that the tumor is growing. Duplicating cancer cells grow fast, while destroying nearby healthy cells. And those cancer cells are pressing on your brain, which is reacting by causing headaches and so forth. Radiation will shrink the tumor, slow down its growth, thereby reducing the unpleasant side effects. And with luck will keep the tumor from metastasizing."

"Spreading cancer to other places in my body."

"Right." Dr. Namagushi nodded grimly.

Sarah gulped. "That's what the doctor told me, too."

"I don't mean to scare you." He corrected himself. "No, that's not true. I do mean to scare you. Not only will the other symptoms get worse, but you could have seizures as well." He paused for a moment. "I'm going to arrange a series of radiation treatments for you at the hospital."

"Will that cure the cancer?"

"Depends. There's the possibility the cancer could go into remission. However, from what you've told me, and what I know about brain tumors, your chances are not good."

"How about alternative medical care."

"You mean, like fasting, meditation, that sort of thing?"

"Yes, I've been reading about miraculous cures. Some people say…"

"Ridiculous! First of all, there hasn't been enough hard research on so-called miraculous cures. Most of the information has been strictly anecdotal. Secondly, many of the practitioners are quacks preying on desperately ill people."

"I don't know what I should do." She placed both hands on his desk.

"Listen, Sarah. If you had a more benign form of cancer, say skin cancer, then I might encourage you to try other methods. Why not? But you simply don't have the time. This kind of cancer is vicious. So why not get the best treatment we can offer you, and make your life more comfortable?"

"I've been reading a lot. Plus I interviewed a lot of cancer victims when I did a series of articles last year on cancer survivors. To me, their treatment sounded as bad as the disease. Like they were being tortured. I don't want to do something that makes me feel worse than I already do."

Dr. Namagushi leaned over and patted her hand. "It isn't that bad, really. Let me take care of everything," he said in a compassionate voice. "We have medications for the nausea. We can insert a morphine pump for the pain."

But Sarah felt her jaw tighten against her will. "Don't treat me like a child."

The physician looked at the pianist with a question in his eyes.

Jim turned to her. "Sarah, Dr. Namagushi is one of the best doctors on the island. If he tells you to do something, I think you ought to follow his advice."

"Can I think about it for a couple of days?"

"Sure. Just don't wait too long, or it may be too late to have any positive effect," added the physician.

"Don't wait too long," she repeated, thoughtfully.

"Here, sign this release of information so I can contact your doctor on the mainland. Have him fax your files, test results, and so forth."

She signed the release. "How much do I owe you?"

"Nothing."

"Are you certain?"

"Yes, positive." He looked at Jim meaningfully. Then he handed Sarah a slip of paper. "Here are two prescriptions. One for the immediate pain, something else for the nausea, and my card. Call me very soon."

"I will, doctor. Thanks." She shook his hand more warmly than before.

"Don't mention it."

After she had gotten into Jim's car, she said confidently, "Take me back to the resort, so I can get my car."

"Are you sure you're up to driving?"

"I need to go home. Change my clothes. Regroup."

"I'm not sure I should let you drive."

Sarah promptly walked into the rearview mirror of a parked car, banging her side. "Damn it," she shouted impotently at the vehicle, as though it had deliberately jumped in her path and she rubbed the bruised area.

"Forget it, Sarah. Get in."

She climbed in to his car, looking quite despondent, and slammed the door. "I didn't see that car."

"I'll take you to your hotel and you can check out. Then I'm taking you back to my house. I'll leave these prescriptions at the pharmacy before we go."

"I don't really want to," she said firmly.

"If you stay at your hotel, you could need help and no one would know if anything happened to you. I'd never forgive myself."

Sarah wrinkled up her face, her mouth puckered. "I'm tired of you treating me like an invalid."

"Sarah, you're sick," he reminded her.

"I know," she admitted. Then she added, "but I don't want to be!"

"Be reasonable, Sarah."

"I insist that you take me to my hotel."

"Okay, but I'm not leaving your side."

She sighed in exasperation. "You're very pig-headed."

"No more so than you."

She replied, "I give up. Let's go."

Jim smiled broadly and drove to the Sheraton.

Chapter 8

Love In All The Wrong Places

Jim pulled into a drugstore in Poipu, where he had Sarah's prescriptions filled. Then he drove to her hotel, allowing the valet to park his late model silver Mercedes.

Sarah was just unlocking the door, when Jim said, "You need to take these medications right away." Then he walked into her room.

"Yes, doctor," she replied sarcastically.

"I'm just trying to help."

"I wish you wouldn't try so hard."

"Do you want to be sick?"

"Of course not. But I'm used to doing what I want, when I want. Eating and drinking what I want. My body was a perfectly-tuned machine."

"And a lovely machine it is, too."

She glared at him. "I'm taking a shower and changing my clothes."

"Need any help?"

She ignored his off-color question, went into the bathroom, closed and locked the door.

Jim turned on the TV, tuning in the station that played only music. Then the tired man slipped off his oxfords, peeled down the bedspread, plumped up a couple of pillows, and lay down, closing his eyes. Within a minute he was asleep and snoring.

Sarah popped several of the pills from the plastic containers into her mouth, washing them down with a gulp of water from a glass provided. Then she took a long, luxurious shower, letting the hot water stream over her. As the water flowed along her body, Sarah remembered another's recent touch. As she lathered her body, brushing her breast with the tip of a finger, Sarah imagined it was his hand instead.

"What's Lani doing right now? He should have returned home by now. Or is he with some attractive woman from the conference?" She rinsed off the soap, but a few meandering suds made her eyes sting. "What if he never comes back to me?"

The depressing idea made her headache worse. A patchwork quilt of thoughts and feelings accumulated in her uneasy brain, making her apprehensive. This new sensation, not caused by her illness, pierced her core, and she touched her chest uneasily, fingering an old torment. "Abandonment is not an easy thing to live with. I don't like it. I don't want it. Why do men leave me? I don't want Lani to leave me." The pain increased. "He can't leave me. It wouldn't be fair." She turned around, the water splashing her back, and put her hands against the tiled wall, momentarily forgetting the shower. "What would I do if he left me?" She thought about the laughing Polynesian. "But we didn't make any promises. No commitments. There hasn't been time." She grimaced, bitterly. "Time. No time." She used the word "time" as if it was a mantra, only it tortured instead of soothed.

The bathroom swirled thickly with steam, but Sarah was oblivious, a prisoner of her frightening thoughts.

"No." She fought hard, her positive attitude winning over her negative beliefs. "I don't know anything for sure. I'm just scaring myself. I figure I have at least a fifty-fifty chance that he'll come back to me." Feeling stronger and surer, Sarah shampooed her hair, rinsed, and stepped out into the dampness of her bathroom.

As she stepped into the adjoining bedroom, she heard snoring over the music from the television. She toweled dry her hair, peeking around the corner. Jim was curled up on her bed, fully dressed, sleeping off his exhaustion of the night before.

She chuckled and shook her head. She slipped on some shorts and a cotton top, returning to the bathroom to brush out the tangles from her long hair and apply make-up to her pale face.

The drugs were having a beneficial effect; her head hardly hurt at all and her vision was clearer. Furthermore, her insides were complaining loudly, and she realized all she had to eat so far was a banana. She found the menu from room service and browsed through it. "Soup might be good," as she assessed the condition of her unruly stomach.

She heard a sound and looked over at the bed. Jim was stretching, making loud noises as he did so. "How long have I been asleep?"

"Not long. Maybe an hour or so."

"I sure needed it."

"I guess you did. Are you hungry?"

"Yes, I am."

"I'm calling room service. What would you like?"

He walked up to her and read the menu, looking over her shoulder. "Mmmm. You smell good." He generously kissed her on the back of the neck.

"I'm having soup and some toast," shrugging off the touch of his mouth.

"What do they have?"

She pointed to some items on the menu.

"Turkey on sourdough. And lots of coffee."

Sarah called the number and put in their order. Jim was still hovering behind her, making her nervous. She got up and sat on the bed instead.

He sat in the chair she had just vacated and yawned. "I'm terribly wrinkled," he commented as he looked down at his clothes.

"Not from where I'm sitting," she replied. "Have you always been so neat?"

"Always. It drove my wives nuts."

"Wives?" she questioned.

"I've been married three times and divorced twice. The third one died." His expression changed dramatically for a moment, as though remembering. Then he brightened. "I really love women." He leaned back in his chair, putting his hands behind his head. "My first wife told me, when we were divorcing, that I must hate women." He snorted. "I think I only hated her."

"How many women have you known?"

He stopped, looked at the ceiling, trying to calculate. "I've lost count. Hundreds. Maybe thousands." He saw Sarah's astonished look and laughed. "It's not as bad as it sounds." He got up. "Excuse me for a moment. I have to go out to the car and get something."

When he returned, he found that room service had delivered their lunch. He waved his swim trunks at her. "You should get some fresh air after we eat. Will do you good."

"You're the boss."

After eating they got into their beach attire and settled into chairs on the beach.

"This isn't too sunny for you, is it?" he asked, adjusting the beach umbrella over her.

"Not too bad. I need some sunscreen."

"I meant, for your general health."

"Oh, that," she replied, with disgust in her voice. "What a pain, having to think about..."

"Do you need help putting on the sunscreen?" he said, changing the subject.

"Just on my back."

"Here give it to me." While Sarah held her long hair up out of the way, Jim slowly spread the slippery substance over her fair skin, around her bikini. He lingered over her shoulders, rubbing the lotion in sensuous circular movements, kissing the back of her neck, under her hair.

"Stop it!" she demanded.

He acquiesced and lounged in the chair next to hers, his long tanned legs stretched out casually in front of him, looking elegant as usual.

"Did you iron your swimming trunks?"

"No. Why do you ask?"

"They look starched and pressed."

He laughed. "I'm meticulous but I haven't ironed my trunks. They're new."

"Oh." She applied the sunscreen on her arms, legs, stomach, face, and was just starting on her chest.

"Need assistance?" he asked, coyly.

"Mind your own business," she retorted.

"Just trying to be helpful."

"Um, hm," she said, rolling her eyes. "You know, you don't have to sit here, keeping me company. Wouldn't you rather be surfing or chasing women or something?" she asked caustically. She screwed the cap back on the sunscreen and put it in her canvas bag.

He squinted at the waves. "Not very good surfing here. Kealia beach is better." He pointed out at the wild breakers. "Besides, I want to be with you."

An immediate pall fell over her. "Wouldn't you rather be with some-one who's well?"

"You don't seem too sick right now."

"That's an awful thing to say."

He hung his head. "I'm sorry, Sarah. I don't know what's the matter with me. When I'm around you, my tongue and my brain get all twisted up, and I say or do stupid things. Not like me at all."

"How are you usually?"

"Generally I'm very diplomatic and well-bred. At least, that's what all the women say."

"All the women," she repeated, with irony.

"I told you, I really love women."

"So how does one go about finding these thousands of women?"

"It's not hard in Kauai. My job is a perfect place to meet women. A lot of them make passes at me. Old ones. Youngish ones. They come up to me when I'm playing, sometimes shyly, sometimes aggressively." He smiled shrewdly.

"You seem very sure of yourself."

"It's like falling off a rock. When a woman is vacationing in para-dise, she doesn't have a lot of time. She finds herself wanting to fulfill all her fantasies of utopia, so she allows herself to be open to any im-mediate action. And there I am, playing the piano, and singing love songs every night." He yawned, still tired from his interrupted night's sleep.

"You sound very callous."

"Not at all. Every woman wants romance in her life. And Kauai is romantic with a capital R."

"Is that what I am to you? A woman looking for romance?"

"No. You're different. Remember that I came up to you."

"That's right."

"I felt compelled to talk to you."

"Why? When you have hundreds of women to pick from, you chose me. I'm not even interested in you."

The barb stung his male ego. "You don't have to remind me." His eyes glittered and he pursed his lips. "Maybe I like the challenge."

"Is that the usual case?"

"There isn't any usual case. You make me sound like a Don Juan."

"Well..."

"But, I really love these women," he said, defensively.

"Sounds to me you enjoy being in charge."

"That's true. There's an element of control that I have."

"How can a woman have a romance with you during such a short time?" and she thought about her own situation.

"I can break through most any woman's inhibitions quickly. She knows she's going home soon, and doesn't have much time to waste."

"Not much time to waste." she echoed.

"So I become part of her vacation. Something to put in her scrapbook, along with the photographs of the beach and the mountains."

"Kauai's natural treasure."

"Something like that," he laughed ironically "Fortunately, or unfortunately, I hardly ever hear from any of them again.

"It's a dirty job, but somebody's got to do it."

"There's nothing wrong with a little romance. Nobody gets hurt," he added defensively.

"So, do you have a revolving door to your bedroom?"

"No, we usually go to the woman's hotel room. In her own space she can let her hair down, be safe with me. She knows she can always call the front desk and have me thrown out if I'm not the man she hopes I'll be. Later she can tell her girlfriends back home about our affair, and they'll giggle with envy."

"It almost sounds calculated."

"But, you know, I'm getting tired of all that. I'd like to be with a woman on a permanent basis again. Do nice things with her. Cook for her. Make love to her all day." He made a face. "Plus AIDS puts a crimp in one's lifestyle." He hastened to add, "of course, I always practice safe sex."

"The sun's making me dizzy and my head hurts again," she interrupted.

"Let's go in." Jim gathered up their belongings and they headed for her room.

"You must think I'm foolish, spilling my guts to you," he added, as they walked.

"No, I'm used to it. Remember, I used to be a reporter. People confide in me all the time."

"But I'm not used to it. Usually people tell me their secrets."

Sarah unlocked the door and Jim closed it behind them.

She went into the bathroom and changed back into her shorts and top. "Sounds like you're ready for a committed relationship," she continued, when she came out.

Jim sat at the table near the window. "Yeah. The game was fun and exciting for a long time, but I'm getting bored lately. I'd like some special woman whose lovely face I can wake up to every morning. Drink our coffee together and read the paper. Watch the sun set every night with my arm around her. Share a life." He gazed at her lustfully. "Do you know what I mean?"

"Doesn't take a rocket scientist to understand."

"Don't you want someone special?"

"Of course. I don't hate all men."

"Just me."

"I'm sorry, Jim."

He got up and came over to kiss her.

She turned her head away. "No, Jim."

"Damn. I hate unrequited love."

"Do you love me?" She sounded surprised.

"Yes, I guess I do. A little," he said, sitting down next to her. He picked at the bedspread, smoothing out the fabric.

She touched his hand magnanimously, relenting. "Forgive me. I can be a bitch sometimes."

"I don't want to forgive you. I want to make love to you." His erection showed through his trunks. He crawled onto the bed, stroking her face. His face was flushed, his pupils were dilated, and he was breathing rapidly. "Kiss me, Sarah."

She allowed him to kiss her briefly, but his lips felt barren, and she pulled away. "No, this is wrong."

"Sarah," he sucked in his breath. "I'm on fire." He tried to put his arm around her neck.

"Please don't make it worse." She pushed him away. "You've been so kind to me. But…"

"But?"

"I don't love you. I'm not even interested in you."

"Maybe you could, after a while. When you get to know me."

"I don't think so."

"I'm a patient man. Just tell me you'll try."

Lani, she thought. *Lani, where are you? I need you.* Out loud she said, "I can't."

Jim attempted to kiss her again. He took her hand and placed it on himself. "Touch me, Sarah," he whispered.

She moved her hand as if she had been burned. Sarah ached with unsatisfied yearnings, but knew she wouldn't succumb to the blonde man's seduction. "What you ask is impossible." She moved angrily away.

Then she rolled off the bed, intending to phone the front desk. But she was dizzy, staggering from the intense pressure in her head. "Oh, I hate this! Why does it have to be happening?" she cried out. "Why me?" She swayed on her feet, leaning on the small table.

Jim came over to her and tried to put his arms around her, to support her. "Come here, darlin'. Let me take care of you. It'll be all right," he said, trying to soothe the distraught woman.

She pushed him away. ""No, nothing is going to be all right ever again. Get away from me." She gagged and stumbled to the bathroom.

Jim stood in the doorway, while the woman knelt on the cold tile over the commode, violently sick. Minutes later she collapsed on the floor.

He gently picked her up and sat down on the bed with her, still cradling her in his arms. His eyes were sympathetic. "Sarah. Speak to me."

She was limp in his arms, whimpering like a child. Terror-stricken, she looked into his face. "Am I really going to die?" She threw her arms around his strong and healthy body and buried her head in his shoulder.

"Shhh, baby." He rocked her in his arms.

"I don't want to die," and her body shook with sobs.

Jim held her until her crying spell passed and she was calmer. "We've got to go now, honey, so I can get ready for work."

"I'll stay here."

"No," he shook his head resolutely. "I'm not leaving you alone. Bring along some of your things and we'll go back to my place."

"I'm not used to being ordered around," she replied weakly.

He set his mouth firmly and his blue eyes got steely. "Will you walk or should I carry you?"

"I'll walk."

"Don't forget your medications."

"Okay, okay." She picked up a few possessions, the prescription bottles and some of her toiletry items and threw them in her canvas bag. "I'm ready."

After they got in Jim's Mercedes, Sarah's phone began to ring in her hotel room, but no one was there to pick it up.

"Sorry, sir. No answer," said the desk clerk.

"Thanks," replied Lani and hung up without leaving a message. "Shit!" and he punched a nearby pillow.

Chapter 9

Apparitions

Jim got dressed for work while Sarah lay down in the small bedroom again. He brought her a glass of water. "Take your pills now."

"Whatever you say, doctor," she wisecracked but did as she was told.

"You must be feeling a little better." He smiled. "I've left some soup and crackers in the kitchen. Will you need anything else?"

"Don't think so."

"Here's the number of the hotel in case you need me. I'll be back as soon as I can. You should sleep. I promise I won't disturb you."

"Thanks," she replied, calmer now.

After he had gone, Sarah locked the door behind him and picked up the phone directory. "Kamalani Waikoloa. What was the name of that town? Oh yeah, Hanalei. Here it is. 555-3231." She wrote it down then dialed on her cellphone, her hand shaking. The phone rang a number of times, then the answering machine clicked on.

"Hey, bro, hang loose. Can't reach me, 'cause I've gone surfing. You know what to do."

"Lani. Are you there?" She waited a moment, in case he was home, and continued. "This is Sarah. Call me when you get in." She looked in the phone book again. *M. Waikoloa. This must be it.* She called Lani's grandparent's house.

Lani's grandmother answered the phone. "Helllooohoo?" she said, in her lyrical voice.

"Mrs. Waikoloa?"

"Who's this?"

"Lani's friend, Sarah. We, uh, met the other day."

"Oh…sure. I remember you, honey. Long red hair like Pele."

"That's me."

"How you been?"

"I've been okay, Mrs. Waikoloa, " she lied. "How are you?"

"Oh, fine. Hold on a minute." She put down the phone.

Sarah could hear her open the screen door and speak to someone, then slam the door again. She waited for the old woman to return.

After a few long moments, the elderly Hawaiian was back on the line. "You still there, honey?"

"Yes, I'm here, Mrs. Waikoloa."

"Call me Moana. Mrs. Waikoloa is too formal." She chuckled. "Oh, oh." She put the phone down again.

Sarah could hear crackling in the background, like something frying, and the woman mumbling to herself.

"I'm back."

Sarah felt weary and frustrated at the delays and decided to get right to the point. "Mrs. Waikoloa."

"Moana."

"Yes, Moana. I haven't heard from Lani in a few days and…"

"Me, neither," the Polynesian woman interrupted. "I was thinking maybe I should worry. But Mamu says he's fine. Lani always calls eventually. He just loses track of time."

"Is he still in Honolulu?" Sarah pressed her.

"I don't know. Maybe. I never know with Lani." She looked out the window. "His truck's not here."

"Do you know what hotel he's staying in?"

"I think he might be staying with some friends," she replied vaguely.

"Oh." Sarah sighed. "When you hear from him, would you tell him to call me?"

"Sure, honey. Does he have your number?"

"Yes."

"If I hear from him, I will be sure to have him call you. Are you feeling better since you got sunstroke?"

"It wasn't sunstroke, Mrs....uh, Moana."

"Oh? I was sure Lani said something about that. You were really sunburned. And your skin is so pale, gotta be careful. Lani should know better than to take a white girl out too long," Mrs. Waikoloa rambled on.

"I'm going now," Sarah said firmly.

"See you soon, honey."

"Yes, I'll talk to you again, Moana."

"Take care of yourself, now."

"I will."

"Oh, before I forget. We're having a party for Mamu, to celebrate his birthday. I'll tell Lani to bring you. It's this Wednesday night. Big luau."

"Thank you, Moana. That's very kind of you. I'd like to come."

"That's arranged, then. Good-bye, honey."

"Good-bye, Moana." Sarah fell back into bed without bothering to turn off the lamp, exhausted by her conversation, and frustrated at her inability to contact Lani.

As she lay she went over and over everything Lani had said to her, every touch, every look, replaying the memories like an old cassette tape, then rewinding and playing them again. "Oh, Lani, Lani. Why aren't you with me at this moment?" She breathed deeply, as though sheer willpower could make him magically appear in bed with her. Her face flushed with the heat of her longing.

"I should research some more." She thought about the doctor's words and her heart began palpitating. "I can't rest because my heart keeps jumping around. Why am I so agitated? I'm tired and can't breathe, but I can't lay still either." She struggled out of bed and opened a nearby window.

A sharp gust of wind blew through the open window, flinging the curtains aside which knocked over the lighted table lamp.

She muttered and bent over to retrieve the lamp; the bulb had shattered with the fall. "Oh, the hell with it," and she let it stay where it was and lay down again.

A pale ghostly light suddenly appeared in the center of the darkened room. *What's that?* she thought. *My eyes must be playing tricks on me again.* She blinked hard to focus.

"Sarah." A deep, resonant voice emerged from within the light. "Sarah," it said again, more insistently.

"Who's there?" she squeaked in fright.

"Sarah, why didn't you tell Lani you're sick?"

"What?" she cried out and sat up in bed, trembling. "Who are you?"

"You both have much to do and little time to do it."

"I don't understand. What do you mean?" She clutched at the bedspread, beginning to feel panic. The cellphone was across the room on the desk, too far to reach and the eerie presence was blocking her way.

"When I touched your head, I could sense the sickness spreading." She recognized the low, deep bass voice.

Sarah was shaking so hard, so could hear her teeth chattering. "Mr. Waikaloa? Is that you?"

"Come to me soon and I will help you." Then the light disappeared as quickly as it had emerged.

Sarah was dripping wet from fear. After a few moments when nothing more had happened, she cautiously got out of bed and made her way through the dark to the wall and clicked on the light. The room looked perfectly normal, except for the fallen lamp. "What was that?" she asked out loud. "I must be hallucinating now." She thought briefly of going to the emergency room but realized her car was still parked back at the resort where Jim was working. She turned off the wall light, Staggered across the room and turned on the light in the bathroom. Climbed back into bed, pulling the covers up to her nose. The trembling was beginning to subside. She had never felt so alone and scared as she did now. Even the sight of Jim would be welcome.

Sarah Arlington turned over on her side and forced herself to sleep, but fitfully, waking often until the morning light appeared. Then in the rational light of day, she slept soundly.

Meanwhile the phone in her hotel room in Poipu rang insistently and often.

Chapter 10

Fern Grotto

At 11:30am Jim breezed into the room. "Good morning, darlin'. Sleep well?"

"Oh. Good morning," she replied, yawning and stretching, rubbing the sleep out of her eyes.

"I wish you wouldn't act so enthusiastic seeing me," he said humorously.

She yawned again.

He sat on the edge of the bed and took her warm hand. "How are you feeling?"

"Okay," easing her hand away. "I think the pills are helping. I haven't slept this long in ages."

"Good. I thought if you're up to it, I'd take you to see the Fern Grotto today. Get your mind off yourself. Unless you've already been there?"

"No, I've heard about it, though." Her voice sounded more animated.

"Well, I'll take you to breakfast first, then we'll take the boat trip up the Wailua River. That's the only way you can get to the grotto."

"Wailua River? The name sounds familiar."

"Have you been to Opeakaa Falls? It flows into the Wailua River."

"Yes, I have." She blushed with the memory, then picked up her shorts and a cotton blouse and went into the bathroom to get dressed but with a sense of foreboding.

After breakfast at a nearby coffee shop, Jim drove them to the landing where the Alapai family's boats waited to take tourists to the enchanting Fern Grotto.

As they waited for the next boat, a native man with a pockmarked face approached them. He was selling Ti leaf bracelets and anklets. "You want one, lady? It has much mana." He grinned with uneven teeth, but his manner was pleasant.

Sarah said, "I could use some of that mana." She reached for her purse but realized she had left it back at Jim's.

"I'll buy it for you," Jim said. He gave the man a large bill and bought several of the bracelets, one for Sarah and one for himself.

"Thank you," she replied while Jim helped her fasten it on her wrist and put the other one in his pocket.

When the boat arrived, Jim helped her in, ducking beneath the green and white awnings surrounding the three sides. They were the last tourists on the crowded boat, which was packed with sightseers, and took a seat in the middle bench.

Some of the Alapai brothers untied the moorings while the elder Alapai drove the slow-moving vessel up the river. They passed boats from other local companies, all decorated colorfully.

A heavy-set man began playing a twelve-string guitar and a woman he introduced as his sister sang Hawaiian melodies for the tourists during the leisurely tour upstream. Wild plants, trees, and flowers grew abundantly and lavishly on both banks of the river, and after a while the dock disappeared from sight as the boat navigated through the jungle. The guitarist and his sister played and sang beautifully, their strong voices resounding over the chug-chug of the engine.

Sarah was glad of the noise and the music, so she didn't have to carry on a conversation. Jim leaned back against the hard wooden seat, stretching his arm out on the seat behind her. He acted jovial and very sure of himself.

Then two pre-adolescent girls and three older women were introduced. They began to dance a hula on the wooden floor of the boat, accompanied by the man and his sister. Their hand movements were as graceful as the leaves blowing in the tropical wind along the shore. Their bare feet seemed to grip the wooden planks to steady them over the movement of the waves. Their colorful dresses clung to thighs and hips, defining their undulating movements.

When the captain announced they had reached their destination and the flat-bottomed boat was securely moored, the ship's company started filing up the steps up to the pier. The long path leading into the grotto was overgrown with thickly lush plants and trees about twenty feet tall. Wild banty roosters and cats scurried in the undergrowth. Here and there lavish displays of tropical flowers grew.

At least half of the tourists were Japanese, chattering among themselves, herding together into groups to take pictures.

"I should have brought my cellphone," moaned Sarah.

Jim hugged her shoulder from the side. "I'll buy you some postcards." She pulled away from his embrace.

At the end of the path was a steep walkway up to the natural indention, slippery from the water above. The grotto was a perfect growing medium for the many types of ferns growing out of the crevices. Birds had deposited seeds over thousands of years, giving rise to the abundant growth of ferns growing at impossible angles on the stone face and ceiling.

When everyone had gathered at the grotto, the brother and sister team began to sing the Hawaiian Wedding Song. Sarah knew the song popularized on records, but the couple sang it in their native language, their melodious voices reverberating off the steep walls of the grotto. The sweetness of the song and their beautiful voices brought up longing; Sarah's chest ached with bittersweet yearning and sadness. She moved away from Jim, surrounded by the Japanese visitors, still listening in silent awe to the lush notes echoing in the cavern. She could see Jim's blonde head towering above the shorter Asian people and turned away so he couldn't catch her eye. She didn't want to associate him with the song, but thought instead of Lani. Sarah reminisced until the song was finished.

"I knew you'd like it here," Jim smiled once he found her in the crowd.

"Thank you for bringing me. It's more beautiful than anything I've ever seen. And the song touched me profoundly. I don't have words to explain."

"I can tell."

"Are you crying?" she continued.

"Yeah, a little." He wiped his nose. "I'm sentimental, I guess. Plus it reminds me of someone I used to know. We came here on our first date."

"Who is that?"

They started walking down the path, returning to the boat.

"My third wife, Lisa." His teeth were clenched and color flushed his cheeks. A shadow passed over him, darkening his countenance. He dropped the subject abruptly.

On the relaxing boat ride back, he was silent and Sarah didn't press him. The singers and dancers rested, while the tourists milled around the boat, taking pictures, and munching on chips and pretzels from the snack machine on board.

When they got in Jim's car, Sarah questioned him. "Tell me what happened."

"She was a lovely girl, no taller than them." He pointed to the young Hawaiian girls on the dock who had danced the hula. "Hiro introduced us. Lisa was his sister."

"Is that why..."

He continued without answering. "She was beautiful. Smart. Brimming with fun and excitement when I met her. Very passionate, too." He paused.

"And then?"

"A few months after we were married..." He shrugged and continued. "I guess she had been sick for years." He stared at the other cars leaving the parking lot. "But nobody told me and I didn't notice anything wrong."

"What did she have?" realizing that she had asked about Lisa in the past tense.

"Bi-polar. That's why she could party all night." He was silent, thinking of what he wanted to say next. "But then she got very depressed. Just lay around all the time, crying or sleeping. Hiro prescribed Lithium, but she wouldn't take it. I'd find the pills everywhere, in drawers, under the couch."

"What a shame." Sarah began to understand his concern for her.

"One night I came home after a gig as usual. But she had hung herself from the balcony of our apartment."

"Oh, no!" exclaimed Sarah. "Oh, Jim, I'm so sorry." She touched his hand tentatively, but he didn't respond.

His eyes were glazed with emotion. "I did everything I could. I tried to take care of her. I really loved her, but she couldn't see that. The illness." He grimaced. "In the final analysis, I couldn't help her at all."

A car passed them, packed full of children shouting and laughing loudly.

He gazed wistfully at the passing car. "We had talked about having kids."

Sarah stroked his arm.

"The Namagushi's were horrified at the loss of face to their family. They've been trying to make it up to me ever since. Even bought me my house. I think they feel guilty 'cause they never told me…before Lisa and I got married."

"They should have."

"You're right. But I probably would have married her anyway. In those days, I thought I could fix everything." He glanced at Sarah. "Maybe I still do."

"It shows you're a caring person."

"Not necessarily. I think I just want everything in my life to be neat and tidy, well organized, with me in control." He couldn't look at her, and stared straight ahead at the road. "Anyway, after that I started having so many affairs, I couldn't keep count. But it didn't make me feel better."

"How long ago did she die?"

"Three years."

"A long time."

"I think I've finally gotten over her. I'm ready to settle down now. Maybe even have a family, if it's not too late."

She breathed a deep sigh. "If it's not too late," she echoed.

"How are you feeling?"

"Okay."

"The pills are helping, then?"

"They seem to be."

"Good. I'm relieved. You know, you should call Hiro's office, so they can set up your radiation schedule."

"Um, hm," she replied, noncommittally.

"Am I doing it again?"

"What's that?"

"Bossing you around?"

She smiled. "Yes, as a matter of fact, you are."

"Sorry. I can't seem to help it. What I meant to ask you, is, do you feel up to going to the beach?"

"Sure. Why not."

"I think it's healthier than sitting around inside."

"I suppose you're right."

"I'll swing around to my house, I'll change and pick up my board. See if there's any good waves."

"Do you think that's a good idea?" asked Sarah, immediately concerned about meeting Lani there.

"Well, it's not a good time of day, but maybe if we stay long enough…"

"Except that I don't have my bathing suit, or my sunscreen."

"Were you planning to go into the water?"

"No, not really."

"Then I'll just bring some sunscreen along, and you can stay in your shorts."

"Okay," she agreed, but with trepidation.

Jim unlocked his door and stepped aside to let her in. He poured himself a large glass of vodka and slumped on the couch. "I've changed my mind. I don't feel like going to the beach right now."

"That's okay. I'm a little tired myself." Sarah sat next to him. "I'm really sorry about Lisa," she murmured.

He reached for her hand and this time she didn't pull away. "Thanks for saying so. I don't know why I took you to the Fern Grotto. I swore I'd never go back." He gulped down the alcohol.

"Maybe it's time you let go of her."

"I suppose." He got up and measured out another tall drink. "You want one?" Before she could reply, he answered the question for her. "No, you shouldn't. How about some fruit juice?"

"I'd love some."

Jim went into the kitchen and brought back some cold pineapple juice. "This is better for you anyway." He handed her the glass then quickly finished his drink and refilled his own glass once again.

"You know, you're a really kind man. You deserve to find someone who loves you," Sarah told him gently when he had seated himself next to her. She placed her hand on his arm to comfort him. "I understand more about why…"

"But not you," he interrupted morosely.

She couldn't tell if he was asking a question or making a statement. "No," she replied quietly, "not me."

"Why don't you love me?" Jim was beginning to slur his words, the alcohol taking effect.

"Because I, well, I just don't."

"Too bad," he muttered so low she could hardly hear him. He tilted his glass and downed the rest of the liquid. He turned and faced her. "You're incredibly beautiful," he whispered and leaned over aggressively to kiss her.

"Please, Jim," said Sarah. "We've been through this before."

He got up angrily and filled his glass, emptying the tall bottle. He continued to stand at the bar, glowering at her.

"Try to understand," she began.

"Understand what?" he shouted drunkenly. "That I've always felt empty and lonely, no matter what woman I was with. Even Lisa. Maybe she sensed that somehow. Maybe I was responsible for her dying." He laughed humorlessly. "But when I saw you sitting at the resort, with your beautiful red hair blowing around your sweet face, I knew you were the one I had been waiting for my whole life."

"What are you talking about?" Sarah felt disoriented by his violent words and emotions.

He unzipped his trousers and stepped out of them.

"Calm down, Jim. You don't know what you're doing. You're drunk."

"That's right. I'm drunk. But I know what I'm doing."

He stared at her with an expression that frightened Sarah.

She stood up and walked to the door, trying not to anger the man any further but needing to escape.

"I've waited for you a long time, Sarah. I'm not waiting any longer," he muttered ominously and he rushed over and grabbed her by the wrists before she could run away.

"Stop it, Jim! You're hurting me," she cried.

He pushed her down to the floor, then straddled her, pining her hands down with his. Then he kissed her roughly, his tongue plunging deep into her mouth.

Sarah could feel his swollen aggression pressing against her body. She struggled beneath him, kicking her legs wildly, trying to move away. She freed her mouth and screamed. "Jim. Get off me. Stop it!" She tried to fight him off.

He rolled off her, glaring. "You really know how to make a guy feel bad."

She sat up and slapped him hard on the face. A red welt immediately appeared. "Take me back to my room! Now!"

The ugly expression dissolved from his face, replaced with contrition and sorrow. "I'm really sorry, Sarah. I don't know what got into me." He stood up and slowly began pulling on his pants.

Sarah jumped to her feet, shaking with anger and fear.

"Oh, Sarah," he murmured, "I'm so sorry." When he had dressed, he turned to her with the most dejected expression she had ever seen. "Please forgive me, Sarah. This isn't how I normally behave."

"I would hope not!" She stood glaring at him.

"Let me make it up to you."

"No, I just want to leave."

"Please. I'll do anything you ask. Just let me stay with you. I'm nuts about you."

"I can see that!" she said sarcastically.

He reached for her but she flinched. "I went a little crazy, I guess. Going to the Fern Grotto. Remembering Lisa. Being with you. Too much to drink." He passed his hand over his forehead.

"I'll call a cab." Sarah got her cellphone out of her purse.

"I'll drive you home," he said softly.

"No, you're drunk. I'll have a taxi take me to my car."

"I don't know what to say."

"There's nothing more to say."

Jim motioned for her hand but she stood motionless as a stone. "Can we forget this ever happened and start again?"

"I don't know about you, but I won't ever forget!" Sarah cried.

"I'll call you tomorrow," he persisted.

"Don't!"

Sarah picked up her bag and waited outside for the cab, shaking violently. When she got back to her hotel room, she locked the door, and turned on all the lights. She dialed Lani's house but only got his answering machine again.

"Hello, bro…."

She hung up without leaving a message, sat down on a chair, her body trembling relentlessly while her mind was mercifully blank.

After the extended conference that day, Lani thought about calling Sarah again, but he had made up his mind never to call her and went to sleep in his hotel room instead. He dreamt disturbing dreams of dangerous seas and men with scars on their faces.

Chapter 11

Reunion Merry-Go-Round

Early the next morning, after she had gotten dressed, Sarah heard a knock on her door and jumped nervously. She stood indecisively in the middle of the room, trying to make up her mind to answer it. Then she heard another knock.

"Who is it?" she called hoarsely, afraid of what she would hear.

"It's Lani, Sarah."

She ran to the door and flung it open. "Lani!!" she said, then felt suddenly shy in his presence.

Lani's brown eyes bore angrily into hers. "I've been trying to get hold of you for days. Where have you been? I was worried."

Sarah felt a flood of guilt and flushed crimson. "I wasn't feeling well and I haven't been staying at the hotel."

"Every time I called, you weren't in. I even asked the hotel if you'd checked out but they said you were still registered."

"I called the hotel but they told me I didn't have any messages."

"I guess I should have left one."

"I left a message and also talked to your Grandmother."

"I haven't listened to my messages. I haven't been home yet either. I came straight here."

"Sounds like we had our signals crossed."

"Mmmm. Can I come in?"

"Oh, yeah, of course." She ushered him in.

He entered hesitantly. He was dressed casually in a familiar pair of shaggy shorts and a t-shirt with the sleeves rolled up, exposing his muscular biceps. He stood awkwardly near the entrance.

"Sit down."

He perched tentatively in a chair near the window. Sarah sat on the edge of the bed.

"The conference lasted longer than I thought it would. I called you as often as I could but you were never home." He crossed his arms in self-protection, bile rising in his throat, heat starting in his head.

"You've said that already."

"Oh. Right."

She licked her lips and looked around the room, unable to look Lani directly in the eyes.

"I missed you," he said simply.

Sarah's heart jumped a beat and she smiled warmly. "I missed you, too." She could hear him sigh with relief but she was fearful to tell him what she knew she must. Jim and her illness stood between them like an invisible wall.

Lani broke the tension first. He went over to Sarah, sat down and put his arms around her, hugging her to him.

Sarah felt herself melt, feeling safe and reassured in his arms. She lifted her face up to him and let him kiss her. The kiss was soft and gentle. "Ummm," she breathed, as their kiss ended.

"I was afraid...I was afraid..." he whispered urgently in her ear.

"Of what, my love?" she questioned.

"That something terrible had happened."

Sarah pulled slightly away from him to gaze into his eyes. She saw the fear there, a mirror of her own apprehensions.

"You won't leave me, will you?" he asked sorrowfully. "I couldn't stand it." He buried his head in her fragrant hair, having said more than he planned.

Sarah knew she should open up and tell him everything, but she felt exposed and vulnerable and afraid.

Lani felt her hesitation and misunderstood its meaning. He let go of her and stood up. "What is it, Sarah?" he asked hesitantly, looking down at her, needing to know yet troubled by what she might say.

"There are so many things I have to tell you. I don't know how to begin." She bit her lip. "But I can tell you this much, truthfully. I would never leave you if I had a choice."

He wrinkled up his forehead. "What do you mean? Are you being deliberately mysterious?"

"No. Just be patient, while I find the words." She gestured. "Please sit down."

"I'm being as patient as I can." Lani sat.

She took a deep breath and then so did he. "I'm used to being alone. Doing what I want, when I want. But being with you has uncovered a core of hunger in me. I didn't even know it existed. All my cells have come alive with it. All these years I've covered up the hunger with my work, interviewing people about their lives, ignoring mine. My feelings are overwhelming. I can't think. I can't focus on anything productive. All I can think about is you, your face, your body, your lips, your hands touching me. But I'm afraid you'll leave me."

He stood up and reached for her with a look of relief on his face. "Sarah…"

"No, there's more." He bent over and kissed her tenderly, interrupting her. "I know what you mean."

"You do?"

He pulled her up and gathered her in his arms. "I have this crazy notion that if I fall in love, I'll die. So I never got too involved. I've dated some girls, but none of them were like you. No one I've ever met is like you."

She hugged him.

"I think I love you but I don't want to find out for sure. I've even started having my nightmares again."

"What nightmares?"

He hesitated, afraid to reveal himself. Then he took a breath and plunged in. "The ones that began after my folks were killed. Just a series of images. Nothing that makes any sense. A man with a scar. A girl beckons me into the ocean, where I know something dangerous is waiting for me. Next I see my body lying broken and bleeding on the rocks at Lumahai Beach. I always wake up in a sweat. For years I wouldn't go in the ocean."

"Oh Lani. I'm so sorry."

He continued without comment. "My grandfather helped me past my fear, even taught me how to surf. After that, the dreams stopped. But when I was at the conference, the dreams started again. My heart beats so hard when I wake up, it feels like I'm having a coronary."

"Do you think you're just being superstitious?"

"Maybe I am, but better safe than sorry, as they say."

"I think we're a lot alike."

"In what way?"

We're both terribly frightened of love. So we throw ourselves into our work to escape from the fear. But it's also a self-fulfilling prophecy."

"What do you mean?"

"By hiding in our work, we forfeit any love we might have."

"Quite profound, Dr. Freud."

"I've had a lot of time to think lately. Sometimes dreams have important meanings that we're supposed to pay attention to. At least, that's what I've heard. I've had some unusual dreams myself."

"Like what?"

"About the ocean. Death. A man with a scar."

"Really? You, too? I can't believe it!"

"Yeah, a terrible scar down his face. Makes him look deformed, hideous."

Lani inhaled suddenly. "What do you think this means?"

"I don't know." She clung to him. "Maybe because I have…" She stopped. The pain was gathering its forces again and she felt her resolve evaporate.

"Go on."

"Um, having all this happen so fast with you," she finished lamely. Her head was throbbing now.

Lani nodded. "I guess we have what's called a whirlwind romance."

"Excuse me. I'll be right back." She went into the bathroom, closed the door and gulped some of the pills from the two bottles and washed them down with some water. She looked at her wan image in the mirror. "No, I can't tell him. Not yet. What are you going to do, Sarah Arlington?" She splashed some water on her face, brushed her hair and put on some lipstick. "That's better. At least I don't look like the walking dead." She smiled grimly to her reflection. When she returned, Lani was lying on the bed, waiting for her.

"Come here, young lady."

She smiled and cuddled up next to him.

"You know, I have a funny feeling you're not telling me everything."

"Like what?" she stalled, trying to feign innocence.

"I don't know. Am I right?"

"Yes," she said cautiously. "But I can't talk about it right now. It'll have to wait. Okay?"

"Sure. Whatever you say." Then he kissed her sweetly.

Sarah felt her body respond as they pressed their lips together in ecstatic union. For a few moments everything else, including the headache, faded into oblivion.

When they came up for air, she remembered. "Lani?"

"What?" he breathed tenderly in her ear.

"Your grandfather's having a big party tonight, for his birthday."

Lani sat up. "Oh, my gosh. I forgot. I'm supposed to help Gramma get everything ready." He sprang up from the bed and ran his fingers through his hair. "They want me to bring you."

"I know."

He looked puzzled.

"I called their house, to see if they knew where you were. Your grandmother told me I was invited."

"We better get going then. If I know Gramma, I have a lot to do."

"Just give me a few minutes to change and put on some makeup." Sarah was glad of the temporary reprieve.

Within a short while, Lani was speeding down the road, through the tunnel of trees to Hanalei.

Chapter 12

Luau

While Lani got busy preparing the party, Sarah tried to make herself useful, too, but Moana would have no part of it.

"You're a guest. Go sit down. I'll bring you some lemonade. Or would you rather have a beer?"

"Lemonade is fine," and she made herself comfortable on a chaise, out of the way. At the beach across the street, Sarah could hear the surf crash against the rocks at the shoreline. Within a few short hours, the Waikaloa property was transformed into a Polynesian fantasyland. Lani strung up tiny, twinkling lights around the yard and lit torches, which smoked. The wind rustled through the trees and blew the smoke into her eyes.

"Sorry," Lani said, as he adjusted the torches. "That's better," and he dashed off again.

Several chickens pecked in the dirt, clucking nervously, ready to go to roost. A determined-looking woman followed them, wielding a large hatchet. The scent of cooking meat joined in perfumed aromas with freshly cut flowers. Mrs. Waikaloa and her female relatives piled mountains of food on the wooden tables assembled for the occasion

The elderly Kahuna birthday boy came up to Sarah with a bottle of beer in one hand and a flower in the other. He was already inebriated and his eyes were shining. She could have sworn he was still wearing the same baggy pair of jeans and cap that he had on when she met him. He had on a different shirt, though, and a garish tie with dancing hula girls on it. Sarah suppressed a giggle.

He clumsily arranged the flower over one of her ears. "This means you are available," he explained. "Maybe, if Lani gets tired of you, you come see me, eh?" he continued playfully.

His wife had set down a tray of food on a nearby table and waddled over. "It's his eighty-second birthday, Sarah. My honey man just turned eighty-two," and gave her husband a bear hug, enveloping him with her huge body, then she scurried back to the kitchen.

"Happy birthday, Mr. Waikaloa."

The old man planted a very wet kiss on Sarah's cheek and wandered off. She waited until he was out of sight to wipe her cheek dry. Sarah thought about the mysterious vision and was glad he didn't mention anything.

Musicians started setting up. It was the same Alapai family that had played at the Fern Grotto only two days before. Sarah felt her face go hot. "I hope they don't recognize me," she thought.

The older male singer paused as he was tuning his guitar and waved to her. "Hi, there. I hope you enjoyed your tour of the grotto."

"Very much, thank you," she said quickly, hoping Lani wasn't listening. Fortunately, he was nowhere to be seen.

Men and women in colorful clothes began arriving, talking and laughing. All the woman wore leis. Sarah had never seen so many different kinds. Some of them had unique tiny blue flowers interspersed with plumeria or orchids. Sarah got dizzy from the overpowering perfume as she was introduced to and hugged countless friends and relatives of the Waikaloa family.

Lani's aged Auntie hobbled over to talk to Sarah. "You like the poi?" She held up a large ceramic bowl filled to the brim with the purplish substance.

"Well," said Sarah, "I haven't tried it yet."

That's two-finger poi. Made it myself."

"Two finger?" Sarah looked puzzled.

"Depends on how thick you make it. Very thin, three finger poi. Not so thick, like this, two finger poi. One-finger poi, very thick, very good. Here, you try," and helped her dip into the concoction.

Sarah tried not to make a face.

"No like? Better you eat with roasted pig later."

"Okay, I will."

"You see. You try other things. Good too."

Lani's auntie limped away, pleased with herself.

Daylight was waning and the full moon was emerging over the eastern horizon when Lani appeared again, having first changed out of his clothes. He was dressed only in a piece of cloth wrapped tightly around his waist and thighs. His wide bare feet displayed an evolution meant for climbing palm trees or gripping a surfboard. His torso was naked and shining with sweat. Around his neck was a necklace of large black seeds tied in back.

Sarah quickly looked around, then tentatively touched his gleaming chest, running her fingers over his muscles.

"Don't worry, honey. Nobody is watching—directly. They all have a game of watching out of the sides of their eyes. Very native. You get privacy and they enjoy the scenery. Clever huh?"

"Very clever, and quite polite."

"In a society where everyone was naked and making love on the beach, you learned to not look."

"Hm."

"How's it going?"

"Well, I've been indoctrinated into the poi."

"Good old Auntie. Do you like it?"

"I might get the hang of it."

"Watch out, though. It'll make you fat, like gramma."

"Really?"

"It's chock full of vitamins. They add it to baby food, too."

"No way."

"It's true."

A young woman ran up to him. "Granny wants you to help her with the pig."

"Pardon me. Duty calls." In a special ceremony, his cousins helped Lani take the roasted pig out of the ground and transport it to a table. Then he pulled off the layers of tapa leaves, removed the bones and fat and cut it up. The guests clapped and shouted in appreciation.

Mrs. Waikaloa lumbered up to the front of the group. "Come on, everyone. You eat now."

The guests didn't have to be asked twice and they lined up immediately. Tables were bulging with food. Fresh pineapple spears, papaya and mango slices, coconut chunks, and a whole sliced watermelon. Smoked ahi and the ceremonial pig of course. Pieces of cold marinated mahimahi, and sashimi, pickled cucumbers and sliced pink octopus, tasting like sweet turkey. Macadamia nuts and the lavender two-finger poi, sweet Hawaiian bread, plus kegs of beer and pitchers of mai tais. Strong aromatic Kona coffee was brewing, but nobody was drinking it yet.

Children ran around, giggling noisily, playing and teasing each other.

The guests got busy eating while they talked, laughed, and joked with each other.

Lani motioned to Sarah and together they selected morsels from the various tables and sat down to eat. He dipped his finger into a purple puddle on his plate and stuck it in his mouth.

He picked up a small piece of the roasted pig, dipped it in the poi and offered it to Sarah. She opened her mouth and he inserted it. "That's delicious," she murmured.

"Good poi, Auntie," he called out.

Sarah could see the old woman beam with delight and was glad to be in the loving circle of his family.

The musicians had finished eating and were tuning up their instruments. Lani jumped to his feet.

"You're not done," Sarah pointed out.

"Can't eat when there's music playing."

The Alapai family started playing and a number of people started dancing to the music.

Sarah realized how little she knew the handsome Hawaiian man. Lani was very graceful and limber, matching the beat of the instruments, sliding across the ground in time to the music with his wonderfully flat expanse of feet. His sensuous grace added to his powerfully masculine body, with the sinewy muscles, gleaming black hair, and dusky skin shining with sweat, making her achingly aware of her physical longing for him.

Sarah was entranced and mesmerized by the drums with their insistent beat as brown-skinned people, adults and children alike, moved in ritualized steps and a suggestive manner. The women's hair floated around them like dark veils and their bodies breathed with sensual mystery. The scent of many flowered leis perfumed the air.

Sarah felt chillingly alien, aware of her pale white skin and ignorant of their culture.

Then the rhythm changed to a faster tempo and the other instruments were quiet, while only the drums spoke. The tall Hawaiian suddenly became a warrior, leaping in an ancestral dance, moving in ancient movements, at once desirable and unattainable. The drums pounded and her heart pounded with them in rhythm to the handsome man in front of her, joined now only by male friends and family. He didn't smile, but was deadly serious as he concentrated, slapping his thighs in time to the music, moving his legs and arms, his body lost in the ancient dance. The drums beat faster still and so did Lani and the other participants, while the insistent beat went on and on. One by one the other men sat down, panting and wiping away sweat, until finally only Lani was on his feet. People clapped their hands or beat their thighs, shouting and whistling as he spun around like a whirling dervish. Sweat poured down his chest and he merged with the land, the ocean, the flickering torches. The pounding moved to her temples and it seemed that she could feel the drums in her chest, throbbing and pounding with passionate emotion until she felt that her heart would burst. Finally the wild tune ended and everyone applauded enthusiastically while Lani grinned in acknowledgement, breathing heavily.

The musicians began playing another tune, slow and seductive. He came over to Sarah, arms outstretched, beckoning to her.

"I can't," she mouthed.

"I'll teach you." He grabbed her hand and led her protesting to the middle of the dancing area. Sarah followed his lead, attempting to move her body in rhythm to his. Lani expertly danced in front of her, now close, then far, his seductive hips and thighs teasing and tantalizing her. Sarah found herself imitating him, moving her body in ways she only vaguely remembered later, while the hypnotic pulse of the music excited and stimulated her. Her body began to communicate with his through movements as natural as breathing. She forgot the other people around them and made love to Lani through her dance steps, gliding and undulating on a bed of music. Their eyes were locked in a dizzying embrace. She felt him caressing her breasts, heaving with emotion, although he never physically touched her. He danced around her and she found herself getting light-headed in the moonlight. Lani's body became luminous and ephemeral and she blinked her eyes to bring him into physical focus. The drums beat louder inside her head. She heard a loud buzzing sound and everything started spinning around her. Her breathing became heavy and labored. Sarah swayed, unsteady on her feet and reached for him, but her hands found only air. Then suddenly she toppled to the ground,.

Several women screamed and the musicians stopped at once. Lani rushed over to her and picked up her limp body in his strong, moist arms. Then he carried her to his house a few hundred feet away. Someone was there ahead of him, opening the screen door.

"Thanks, cousin," and Lani strode inside, his bare feet making slapping sounds on the linoleum floor. He walked across the room and laid her gently on his bed. "Sarah." She wasn't moving. He leaned over and could hear her faint breathing. "Sarah," again he called her name, more urgently now. He lightly slapped her cheek, trying to revive her.

After a few moments she opened her eyes slowly. "What?"

"You must have fainted," Lani explained.

"Oh, no. Not in front of all those people," Sarah murmured.

"Are you all right?"

She tried to sit up but fell back to the pillow. "I'm okay," she assured him. "I can't believe I fainted in front of all those people," she repeated. Her head still throbbed and her body trembled.

"You must tell him now," a deep bass voice said behind Lani.

Lani turned to his grandfather, who had followed him into his little house. "Tell me what?"

"She knows what I mean. Don't you, Sarah?"

Sarah closed her eyes, unwilling to face either man.

"Would someone please tell me what is going on?" implored the young Hawaiian.

The Kahuna walked over to his grandson and looked at him through bloodshot eyes. The light from outside flickered in through the small windows, illuminating his wrinkled face. The elder's hawk-like eyes seemed to pierce the near-darkness. "Sarah is very sick. Something is in her head."

"A growth," she said very quietly, apologetically.

"I am right, then?" asked the elderly man.

"Yes, you're right."

The older man walked over to her, stared down at her face and then he put his hand firmly on her forehead. "I've been having dreams and visions about you every day since I met you. Always there is blackness around you. Without help you are not meant to walk long on this earth."

Hearing his grandfather's words, Lani gasped. "Sarah, tell me it's not true."

"Please don't lie to my grandson anymore," and with that the old man left and returned to his party. Outside, they could hear him explain to his guests that Sarah was fine. The music began again.

Long minutes went by before Sarah could muster the courage to talk. "It's true, Lani. I was afraid to tell you. I'm sorry. I didn't mean to hurt you. I was scared that you..." She changed the subject. "Your grandfather is amazing."

"He's uncanny, isn't he?" But Lani's eyes demanded an explanation.

"Totally amazing." She looked away, contrite and ashamed.

"What is it?"

"Cancer," she said so softly that he had to lean forward to hear her.

"Oh, no," he exclaimed. "Oh, Sarah, no. It can't be true." He paced around the small room in distraught circles. "Why didn't you tell me?"

"I'm sorry. I wanted to tell you. I meant to tell you." She faltered. "But I couldn't."

"Why?"

"Please don't be angry."

"I'm not angry. I'm upset."

"At first I didn't want to say anything because I didn't know you. I thought we'd spend a little time together and then you'd be gone. No need to explain…"

"…because what we had wasn't serious," he prompted her

"Yes. But…"

"…it didn't turn out that way."

"No. And then I didn't know what to do. I didn't want to hurt you. Or me. I don't know." She looked at him, begging forgiveness with her eyes. "I kept hoping the cancer was just a terrible dream and I'd wake up."

He came over, sat down and put his hands on her shoulders. She rubbed her cheek against one of them.

"Oh, Sarah. I would have understood. I do understand. I'll take care of you."

"I don't want your pity." She pressed her lips thinly together.

"What do you want?"

"I don't know."

"So the other day. At the beach. Your headaches. Your vision problems."

"Yes," she answered, without hearing the whole question.

Lani lovingly stroked her face and she kissed his hand. "Well, at least you've told me now. I knew there was something you were hiding earlier today."

She nodded.

"So what are you doing? Chemotherapy or radiation?"

"I haven't done anything."

"Are you crazy? You have to do something!"

"Please don't shout."

"I'm sorry. I…you're impossible."

She took his hand. "Don't be angry at me. I didn't want to have to go through that awful treatment."

"But you're sick."

"I know," she reluctantly admitted.

"Are you going to die?"

Sarah sucked in her breath hard. "That's a possibility."

"But you can't." He knelt down and laid his head on her stomach, only now fully realizing the impact of all she was saying. "You can't leave me."

"It's ironic, isn't it?" she asked. "I was afraid you'd leave me." She sounded calm, almost peaceful. She stroked his wet forehead, pushing back the wild locks of hair from his face.

"I don't think I could stand it," he muttered.

"I didn't plan on meeting you and falling in love," she explained. "I just wanted to come to this beautiful island, to live as much as I could before…"

"That's why Grandfather left the house so quickly the day he met you. He didn't want to tell me."

"Something like that."

"Oh, Grandfather." He groaned, then straightened up. "Grandfather can help you." He almost looked cheerful.

"Help me do what?"

"Heal you."

"Does he do healings?"

"Once in a while."

"Has he ever healed cancer?"

"I don't know. I'll go get him right now."

She held him back. "No, Lani. Let him enjoy his party. Besides, he may not be quite up to healing right now."

"Maybe you're right. Why don't you stay here tonight and he can work with you tomorrow?"

"Okay." She didn't sound hopeful.

"In fact," he brightened up, "I have an excellent idea."

She looked at him, questioningly.

"I was going to ask you…but you probably wouldn't. It's too big a step. I don't want to rush you. And besides…"

"Do I get a chance to participate in this debate?" she asked.

"Well, I thought…that is, it seems like maybe it would be a good idea. Although I don't know…"

"For heaven's sakes, Lani, just spit it out."

"Maybe you could move in with me. No, it's too crazy an idea."

"I think it's a great idea," she responded enthusiastically. If you want to, that is." When he didn't reply immediately, she said, "Of course, I may get worse…"

"That's not what I'm worried about."

"What, then?"

"What if I die, like in my dream?" He laughed a little. "Sounds ridiculous now, doesn't it? I'm not the one fighting cancer." In the glow from the torches outside, she could see his dimples flaring, as he attempted to be charming. "Sarah, would you consider moving in with me?"

"Yes, I'd consider it." She grinned at him.

"What I mean is. Would you move in with me?"

She kissed him fully on the mouth. "Yes, my darling. I would love to move in with you." She looked around at the tiny house. "But is there enough room for me?"

"Actually we'll be squeezed together like two pearls in an oyster."

"Sounds cozy," she agreed.

He moved his head closer to hers, cupped her face with his hand and began to kiss her fiercely.

Electrified waves of energy thrilled through her body at the touch of his lips.

"Lani?" A woman was calling him from outside. "Lani?"

"Coming!" he called. He reluctantly pulled himself away and went to the door. "What is it, gramma?"

"I've got the cake and candles ready. We're gonna sing happy birthday to Mamu now," his grandmother said to him.

"Be right there." He turned to Sarah, smiling broadly. "Are you available for the candle-lighting ceremony? I hope we don't have to call the fire department!"

She laughed merrily. "Of course." She held out her hand, he helped her to stand up, and together they went outside to sing to the aging Kahuna.

Chapter 13

Truth Heals Pain

The next afternoon Lani, Sarah, and Mr. Waikaloa sat at the small table in Lani's house. The Kahuna touched Sarah's head with his gnarled hand. "The darkness has gotten much worse. It's spreading quickly like hot lava down a mountain, destroying everything in its path."

"Oh, no," interjected Lani.

"How can you tell?" asked Sarah.

He shrugged. "My Voices describe things to me. Shhh." He cocked his head, listening. "They say I must tell you a story."

"A story! How will that heal me?" asked Sarah impetuously.

"What kind of story?" asked his grandson, encouraging him.

The old man looked through the window at the greenery outside, his eyes far away and dreamy. "Once, a long time ago, two people loved each other very much. Then they lost each other and their hearts broke. They began to look for each other everywhere, in many times and places. They became desperate with the passage of time that they would never find each other again. They began to choose other lovers to replace what they had lost. But these other lovers were unsuitable. So they remained lonely and unhappy."

Sarah held Lani's hand tightly, listening intently.

The wise man continued. "Then they miraculously found each other again. But they had already given up and their hearts had turned cold, stored safely away, so that they could not be hurt again." He closed his eyes, to see the vision more clearly. "They began to dream bad things. But these were only illusions. Because of their fear, they pushed each other away, the very persons they had been searching for. They put barriers up to keep their hearts safe from being broken again."

Lani squeezed Sarah's hand and looked at her. Sarah could see his misty eyes.

"But they were being tested. Tested to see if they could love each other in spite of the past, in spite of their fears, in spite of jealousy and bitterness and blame. And tested to learn to forgive each other and themselves. When they pass this test, then all will be healed." He opened his eyes. "There is more too, but I'm not told what it is." Mamu stopped speaking. The air was heavy with expectation.

Lani spoke first. "Is this story about Sarah and me, grandfather?"

He looked at his grandson. "The Voices asked me to tell this story. I do not question what it means or how it applies to you. The two of you must interpret it for yourselves." His voice sounded flat and far away.

"Do you mean that we knew each other in another life? Like reincarnation?" asked Sarah.

"I don't know about reincarnation. I have been given the story in order for you to begin your healing."

"What should we do first, grandfather?"

"In your hearts you will know how to proceed." He paused. "And more will be revealed."

"Grandfather, does the story mean that somehow I am involved with Sarah's illness?"

The elderly man shrugged. "You must determine this for yourself. It is part of the lesson, to understand the meaning of the story."

Lani sighed.

The old Kahuna stood up, groaning and rubbing his back. "I'm going to walk by the ocean now," and he left without another word.

"His story made me terribly sad," Sarah said. Her beautiful blue-green eyes were sorrowful, looking like melancholy pools at the bottom of a waterfall.

"I know what you mean. My chest hurts." He rubbed the ache.

"I'm sorry I've gotten you involved in all this."

"Don't say that, Sarah. I love you."

She realized this was the first time he had said that to her. "You do?"

"Yes. I know I'm scared of being in a committed relationship. I'm afraid of loving you. But in spite of that, here I am." He smiled wanly. "Maybe that's part of what the story means. To love even when you're afraid to love."

"I'm afraid, too."

"Of what, sweetheart?"

"That you only feel pity for me, or worse yet, will be repelled as I get sicker. Maybe you won't leave me physically, but emotionally."

"I won't leave you in any way."

"Is that a promise?"

"I can't promise."

"Why not?" she asked, in a child-like voice. "I thought you said you're committed to me."

"Life is too uncertain to promise things. Maybe that's what happened to the two lovers in grandfather's story. Maybe they made promises, but situations happened which made them break those promises. And then they couldn't trust anymore."

"I think I understand what you're saying. To just love and let life happen as it will. To not always be waiting for the other shoe to drop."

"Right."

"I don't know if I can do that."

"Me neither. Would you be willing to try?"

"Yes, if you would," and she snuggled up against his chest.

"I'm willing," and he kissed the top of her head. Then the tall Hawaiian jumped up. "Why don't we collect your belongings and bring them back here right now?"

"Lani, are you sure you want to do this?"

"Yeah, I think so. But it's a big step for me."

"For me, too." She got up and went over to where he stood and put her arms around him.

"Let's go before I change my mind."

"I'm ready."

Lani lounged on the bed while Sarah was in the hotel bathroom packing her toiletries, when there was a loud knock at the door. Lani opened it, thinking it might be a bellboy. Instead he was face-to-face with Jim Diamond.

Both men reacted in shock.

"Is Sarah here?" Jim asked, looking past the Hawaiian.

"Who are you?" asked Lani

"I'd like to ask you the same question. Hi, Sarah," he called out, as she came out of the bathroom.

Sarah angrily came to the door. "What are you doing here?"

"I wanted to see if we're still friends."

She was about to close the door in his face, but Lani prevented her from doing so.

"What's this about, Sarah? Are there more lies?" he asked harshly.

"There's something I've been meaning to tell you, both of you," she began hesitantly.

"No kidding," said Jim and he sauntered into the room, closed the door and leaned against it.

The two men eyed each other warily, like rams about to fight to the death for the right to mate.

"Would you both please sit down? You're making me nervous." Sarah sat by the small table at the window. The light from the window made her hair gleam; the gold highlights in her red hair sparkled.

Neither of them sat down, but glared at each other with open hostility. Lani's slanted eyes were veiled, and Sarah couldn't read his inscrutable expression. His normally open and happy face was darkened and his jaw was so tight that the muscles around his jawbone were clearly tensed.

"The day you left for your conference, I went to the library to do some research on curing cancer naturally. I got hungry and went to the resort at Kapaa for dinner."

"Where I picked her up," interjected Jim.

No, you did not," she protested.

Lani gulped, looking like he would bolt from the room, yet struggling against the impulse at the same time. "And?"

"Well, I got very sick again, and Jim helped me."

"I bet he did," muttered Lani.

Sarah glared at him, but continued. "I was throwing up and so dizzy I couldn't drive. Jim's house was close by and he offered to let me stay there for a while until I felt better."

"Wasn't that nice of him!" he retorted sarcastically.

"Well, yeah, it was," she replied.

"All night?" he questioned.

"Yes, all night," replied Jim, grinning, before Sarah could answer.

"But we didn't do anything," she insisted

"Uh, huh," Lani said, frankly disbelieving her.

"Although I would have liked to," Jim interjected truthfully.

She turned to the blonde man. "Would you please stop?" Then she cleared her throat and continued. "I wasn't planning on staying there. Jim went to work. He's a musician at the resort. I fell asleep in his guestroom. He came home late and let me sleep 'til the next morning."

"I'll bet he did."

"Don't be so cynical, Lani!" she raised her voice, unable to hold her temper anymore. Angry that he was misinterpreting the whole situation. "Like I told you, I had been very ill. Threw up my whole dinner. And couldn't see."

"Why didn't he just take you back to here?" Lani spoke louder, too.

"Because his place was closer. And he wanted to take me to see a doctor the next day."

"A doctor?"

"Yeah, one of my good friends is an internist in Kapaa. I asked him to see Sarah as a favor to me. I took her early the next morning. As it was I didn't get much sleep."

Sarah rolled her eyes; the piano player was determined to exaggerate in all the wrong places. "Jim got home late from work, and then I woke him up at dawn to take me back here. But he insisted I see his doctor first, who recommends radiation."

"I thought you weren't gong to have radiation," said Lani, looking smug.

"I wasn't!" she shouted with frustration. "Not yet, at least. Do you understand what I'm trying to explain?"

"Maybe. Go on," Lani replied quieter, but with misgivings. He crossed his arms over his chest.

"There aren't and haven't been any romantic goings-on between us."

"Not that I wanted it that way," added Jim. "She's a very willful woman who isn't easily seduced. But I'm a patient man. I get my way eventually."

"Jim, shut up," she commanded him.

"I'm just trying to help."

"Why don't I believe that?" she groaned.

"So why the secret?" asked Lani, mistrust dripping in his tone.

"Because I thought you wouldn't understand."

"You seem to have very little faith in me," he said hollowly. "First the illness. Now this."

"I was afraid you would react just the way you're reacting now."

Lani ran his hand through his thick black hair. "You know, when I called you in the middle of the night, I got a funny feeling you were with some guy. I didn't know I'm psychic. Maybe it runs in the family."

"I called the hotel but you hadn't left any messages."

"No, I was hurt and angry and decided to break it off with you. I felt something odd was going on and I didn't want to get more involved."

"So why did you come back to my hotel as soon as you got off the plane?"

"I'm either very dumb or very smart, I haven't figured out which. But I couldn't help myself. The car just seemed to have a mind of its own. It drove me right here."

"I'm glad you did."

"I'm not sure I am."

"Please believe me, Lani," she begged.

He shook his head.

"Isn't this touching? A lover's quarrel," said Jim.

She scowled at Jim. To Lani she added, "And then he tried to rape me."

"Right," replied Lani. He laughed sardonically. "It sounds like you didn't discourage him too much."

"Right after we went to the Fern Grotto," Jim added.

"What?" Lani yelped.

"I forgot that part." She smiled ruefully.

"I guess you did." He headed for the door.

"No, don't go. Remember what your grandfather told us."

"That you shouldn't lie to me anymore?"

"I didn't lie."

"You just didn't tell all the truth!" Lani's wrath erupted. His pride was injured and he wouldn't listen any further. He pushed his way past Jim and left, slamming the door behind him.

"Lani, don't go!" she cried out, running after him. But he drove away before she could stop him.

Sarah returned to her room. "See what you've done," she spat at Jim.

He shrugged and sat down on the bed.

"Get out of here."

But he stayed where he was.

"I'll call security and have them throw you out," she warned him.

"Why, Sarah? I'm all you have left."

"You bastard!!" she screamed and looked around for something to throw at him.

"Have it your own way. I'm going." He calmly got up and adjusted his trousers. "You know where I am, darlin'. Don't wait too long. Time is not your friend, you know." He blew her a kiss and closed the door softly behind him.

"Ooooo, I could kill him," she mumbled to herself, then burst into tears, flinging herself on the bed.

Chapter 14

Treatment

Lani was carrying his surfboard into the yard when Mrs. Waikaloa came up to him. "Where's Sarah?" she asked, looking around.

"Back at her hotel," he replied curtly.

"But I thought she was moving in here with you," said the confused woman.

"No!" he replied.

"Whatsa matter, honey?"

"She can go to hell for all I care!" He wiped his eyes with the back of his hand.

"Did you have a fight?"

"It's over, gramma."

She put her hand on his arm but he shook it off roughly.

"I'm gonna go surf for a while."

"I wish you'd talk to Mamu first," his grandmother coaxed him.

Lani softened and turned to look at her. "I didn't mean to yell at you, gramma. I'm just upset."

"I can see that," she replied tenderly, patting his arm.

"What's all the commotion?" The Kahuna joined them.

"Lani and Sarah had a fight," the old woman explained.

"I was an idiot," Lani added.

The old man looked worried. "Are you gonna surf now?"

"Yeah, it'll help me sort things out."

"No, Lani," his grandfather replied. "I don't think you ought to go out just now. The surf's pretty rough today."

"I don't care," the young man answered hoarsely.

"Not today, Lani." The Elder spoke with authority, commanding him.

The younger Waikaloa considered for a moment. "You can't tell me what to do, grandpa," he announced. "I'm not a kid anymore."

"Not today, Lani," he repeated, gripping his grandson's arm tightly.

"She's been seeing another guy," Lani blurted out.

The shaman stared penetratingly into Lani's eyes, making the young man uneasy. "No, you're wrong, son."

"When we were packing, he came to her hotel. She was fooling around with him when I was at the conference."

"You're mistaken, Lani."

"I saw him with my own eyes."

"Your eyes don't always see the truth."

Lani's hurt and pain bubbled to the surface. "This time you can't use your doubletalk and make it all better," he said bitterly.

"Oh, Lani," said the older man sadly.

"I'm going surfing and that's all there is to it." He hefted the surfboard under his arm and started walking away.

"Remember your dreams," called the Kahuna behind him.

"Listen to your grandfather!" the old woman cried.

Lani hesitated then stubbornly kept going. He got to the highway that divided their property from the beach and stopped. In the distance he could hear the waves viciously beat against the rocks near the sand. The vivid images from his dreams coupled with the Kahuna's concern awakened his caution. He returned to the old couple waiting breathlessly in the yard and set the surfboard down against the wall of his house. "Maybe you're right. I'll go tomorrow." He grinned sheepishly.

His grandmother hugged him tightly, relieved.

The Kahuna's shoulders slumped. "I'm getting old," he announced.

"No, you're not, grandfather," and he affectionately patted the bent back.

He smiled grimly. "You must go back to her, Lani."

"I can't do that, grandfather. And I won't. She lied to me."

"It's fear that kept her from telling you the truth. She loves you."

"You think so?" Lani looked hopeful.

"I know so."

The large woman nodded her head vigorously in agreement. "And you love her, too, don't you, honey?"

He hung his head like a small boy. "Yeah, I do, gramma," he replied quietly.

"Then go call her."

"I'll call her tomorrow."

Mr. Waikaloa shrugged his shoulders. "Do as you think best. But don't wait too long."

"I won't, grandfather."

"Bring her back to see me soon."

"I will, grandfather."

The old couple walked slowly back to their house. Lani could hear the old woman whispering to her husband.

"I better call the office. They're probably wondering why I haven't showed up," and the young man went inside.

Meanwhile, Sarah had recovered from her crying spell. She went into the bathroom and took her medicine, then ran the shower. Steam from the hot water began to fill the small room. She looked at her tear-streaked face in the steamy mirror and spoke aloud to her reflection. "I'm gonna wash that man right out of my hair," she said through clenched teeth. "Is that how the song from "South Pacific" goes?" She grimaced and squared her shoulders.

After she had showered, dried, and dressed, she found the card with Dr. Namagushi's name on it and entered the number on her cellphone. "Hello, this is Sarah Arlington. I'm ready to start my radiation now." She listened. "A cancellation? Two o'clock. It's almost that now. Where do I go?" She wrote down the address of the hospital. "I'll leave now. Thank you." She hung up and noticed her hands were shaking. "How bad can it be?" and she shuddered. Then she picked up her purse, locked the door behind her, and headed to the parking lot.

The stark green walls of the hospital seemed strangely surrealistic in a land so filled with color. A few plants stood near the glass windows, breaking the monotony. She found the radiation department and walked briskly over to the reception desk. "Sarah Arlington. I'm here for my treatment. Dr. Namagushi called." She noticed flowers sitting in a vase nearby.

"Oh, yes, Miss Arlington. You need to fill out some forms first. You can sit over there." The pretty receptionist handed her a clipboard and pen.

After Sarah had filled out and signed the numerous forms, a nurse came in and called her name.

"How are you today?" the middle-aged nurse chirped perkily, as she led Sarah down the hall.

"If I was okay, I wouldn't be here," Sarah rudely retorted.

The nurse was silent.

"I'm sorry. I didn't mean…"

"That's all right, Sarah. I understand." She took her into a small cubicle. "Take off your clothing from the waist up and remove all your jewelry. Here's a gown you can put on."

"Thanks," replied Sarah. She changed and was ushered into a room filled with machines that looked like Dr. Frankenstein was at work.

The specialist and his assistant studied the films that Dr. Namagushi's office had sent over. Then they spent nearly an hour, after shaving the spot, marking the area on Sarah's head and aligning the settings on the electronic machine to correspond with her tumor.

"X marks the spot," Sarah quipped nervously.

"We have to get it exactly right," replied the assistant.

When they were finished, the doctor spoke.

"Now, Sarah, you must lie very still. The treatment will take about fifteen minutes and you mustn't move your head."

"I understand."

They left to return to the safety of their lead-lined room, watching through a small thick window. Sarah felt utterly small and helpless. She lay motionless, repressing an urge to rub her nose. After what seemed an eternity, the assistant returned.

"That's it?" she queried.

"We'll see you tomorrow."

Sarah got dressed and returned to the receptionist. "Is two o'clock a good time for you?" the receptionist asked.

"Yeah, sure," replied Sarah.

"I've made out a calendar for you. You'll need to come five days a week for the next three weeks. Then we take some more tests, to see how you're progressing. If you need to cancel an appointment, call right away. You might feel woozy and tired, so you should rest a lot." She handed Sarah the schedule. "If you have any other problems, call your doctor."

"Okay, thanks. Yes, I will." Mindlessly, Sarah found her way to her car, returned to the empty hotel room, undressed, and got into bed. She fell asleep immediately, physically and emotionally drained.

The room was dark when her cellphone played its distinctive sound, jarring her awake. Sarah picked it up and answered it.

"Hello?" she answered sleepily.

"Sarah?" It was Lani.

"Yes?" She was fully attentive now and bit her lip, unsure and defensive.

"Um…" He hesitated.

"What is it, Lani?" She waited anxiously.

"I, um, that is, my grandfather wants you to come back for more healing."

"Oh," was all she said.

"Should I come get you or do you want to drive here yourself?"

"I don't know," she hesitated, while conflicting emotions washed through her.

"What's the matter? You don't sound too well."

"I started radiation today."

"Oh, Sarah. I'm sorry. Would tomorrow be better?" He was instantly solicitous.

"Today. Tomorrow. Hmm. Doesn't make much difference."

Lani could hear the edge in her voice and took it personally. "Look, Sarah. This wasn't my idea."

The red-headed woman was immediately distrustful. "Tell your grandfather," she said with emphasis, "not to worry about me."

Lani held his anger tightly in check. "I think maybe we should talk, too."

"What for? You made yourself quite clear earlier."

"I was angry and hurt. Confused. But grandfather thinks, that is, I think I should give you another chance."

"Thanks a lot," she replied caustically.

The Hawaiian could feel the distance between them widening. "Sarah, listen to me."

"I'm listening," she replied.

"Maybe I've misunderstood…"

"Maybe," she retorted.

"I'm willing to hear you out. Whatever you have to say." His voice was softer, caressing her bruised heart.

Sarah sat breathlessly, as the earth began to turn on its axis once more.

"Sarah?"

"I'm still here," she said quietly.

"Well, what do you want to do?"

"Why don't you come get me now, before I change my mind."

"I'll be right over."

Sarah slipped on some clothes and lay down again to wait for Lani, weary to the bone.

Chapter 15

Gold Light of Transformation

Lani helped Sarah out to his SUV and she slept during most of the trip back. She was too tired to sit up when Lani brought her into his house. She relaxed on his bed instead, while both men sat on wooden chairs next to her.

"There is another element to the story, to the healing, that I must share with you," began Mr. Waikaloa without further delay, inching his chair closer and gently put his leathery hand on her head.

A soothing warmth emanated from his hand and she closed her eyes. A whirl of shadowy images and faint memories passed through her mind.

The wise Kahuna closed his eyes and listened. "There was a third person, a brother. In the past he was jealous and tried to come between the two lovers but got his heart broken, too. He made a mistake and it must be rectified before the healing can be complete. I see jewels buried in the sand, like diamonds." He asked Sarah, "Does this make sense to you?"

"Yes," she replied, as if in a trance. "The man's name is Jim Diamond."

"Ah!" exclaimed the mystic. "The Voices are especially clear today." He began rocking back and forth, chanting a singsong tune. He paused. "Put your hand on her heart and close your eyes," he told Lani. The young Hawaiian did as he was told. The old man took Lani's free hand in his and continued his song.

The images got clearer. Sarah saw the hut, the one from her dream, and she shuddered involuntarily. The roar of the surf was in her ears and she saw it crash on the beach in relentless rhythm.

A dolphin rose to the surface of the water and it began to talk in the Kahuna's deep voice. "The circle is joined together. What was created at the beginning of time will only continue and grow into the future. On and on in endless cycles and rhythms. The circle was never broken, only in your thoughts and nightmares. Whatever has happened was perfect and so it is now and will always be. The only enemy has been your own fear. You must find the healing light in your hearts."

Then Lani, dressed only in his lava-lava, emerged from the swirling waves. Wordlessly, he took Sarah by the hand and led her to the little hut. He paused, stepped inside, came out with the tapa cloth and placed it lovingly around her neck.

"The darkness begins to lift," the dolphin narrated.

In her mind's eye, Lani led Sarah to a bigger hut, where Jim was waiting outside for them, the nasty scar blighting his handsome face.

"Forgive me, brother," Jim murmured.

Lani touched the scar tenderly. "I forgive you and bless you." He glanced at Sarah.

"Forgive me, too," she said to the blonde man. "I've been a selfish fool." And she kissed him on the cheek.

Then the trio put their arms around each other. Nearby a baby cried but was comforted by the dolphin's presence.

Suddenly Sarah saw a huge cloud of golden light above the dolphin, brilliantly shining like the sun. Its powerful rays spread to them, emanated into and around all of them. The three people seemed to expand in the presence of the light and their bodies began to glow. Shards of light entered her skull. The gold light pulsed throughout her body and she felt its energy bathing her with an intense but soothing heat. A deep, pervasive peace flowed into her.

Then the dolphin, in the Kahuna's voice, began again. "The following instructions are for both Lani and Sarah. See yourself in a circle of the gold light. Now bring in the one you know as your beloved into the circle. Imagine the gold light and let it permeate through and around that person as well."

In their minds, both Sarah and Lani saw this happening.

"Now see the connections between you and your beloved, as cords. Now take a knife and cut all cords connecting the two of you, except for the golden cord connecting your two hearts in unconditional love."

Sarah and Lani did as they were told.

"Bring in more of the gold light. Use this balm to soothe and heal the places where the connections were severed."

The man and woman could feel the soothing light and their bodies responded with peace and joy.

"If any of these cords grow back, cut them again and use the gold light to heal."

Lani and Sarah were immersed deep within the guided meditation and neither spoke.

"Now, thank your beloved for being willing to sever any connections except the one between your hearts."

The two people nodded, almost in unison.

"Now imagine you are still within the circle, the gold light still continuing to stream down into you. Bring in the man who has connections to both of you, the one who has a scar."

They did as they were told, both imagining Jim Diamond within the circle of gold light.

"Bring gold light into that man. Notice the connections between you and him and cut those connections. Cut all of them except the golden cord between your hearts, the connection of unconditional love. Then bring in more gold light to soothe and heal where the connections have been severed."

Both Sarah and Lani felt a deep peace, as they sliced away the cords connecting Jim to themselves.

"Finally, bring in more gold light, to wash away any misunderstandings, any resentments, any problems. Thank that man and allow him to leave your circle."

The two lovers sighed in unison when they were done.

The dolphin spoke once again with a benediction. "The perfection of the universe is known only through love. Find the willingness to rejoice in and embrace life exactly as you find it," and the silvery figure slid beneath the waves.

Lani's house was quiet except for the sound of breathing and the bees humming outside the window.

The old Kahuna spoke in a reverent tone. "The ancient ones have spoken and have brought you gifts." Then he directed his voice only to Sarah. "You will sleep now. Do not return to the hospital for your treatments. The darkness is gone."

"Thank you," Sarah said simply and sighed in contentment. She could still feel the golden rays of light swirling through her body.

The wise old man got up, his bones creaking with age, and crept slowly out of the house.

Sarah could feel his warm hand on her head even after he was gone.

Then she slept deeply for two days without waking, dreaming only of the dolphin and remembering its words to her. When she awoke, she found Lani lying next to her, dozing.

She yawned and stretched.

He opened his eyes. "How do you feel?" he asked her quietly.

Her stomach rumbled ominously. "Hungry," she replied, grinning. "I'm mean…"

"I feel strangely well, almost like a different person."

"That's wonderful," he murmured. "I have great confidence in grandpa."

"He's a wonderful man," she agreed.

"I'll go ask Gramma to fix you something to eat."

"No, not yet," she held him back and kissed him gently. "Forgive me for not trusting you," she said simply.

"Forgive me for leaving you."

"You're here now. And that's all that counts," she replied.

Then they both heard a screen door slam. The old woman ran as fast as she could to his house. "Lani, come quick!" Mrs. Waikaloa cried. "Your grandpa…"

Lani jumped up and followed her, an ominous feeling sharp in the pit of his stomach.

Moana showed him into the bedroom she had shared with the wise man for sixty-two years. The Kahuna looked like he was sleeping quietly on the bed, curled into a fetal position.

Lani felt for a pulse in the old man's cold neck. "He's gone, gramma," and he hugged her.

The woman nodded, huge tears splashing down the fat cheeks. Then she eased herself onto the bed and positioned herself behind her husband, cradling him from behind. She began to keen and rock his dead body. "Mamu," she wailed. "Mamuuuuu."

When Lani returned, Sarah was dressing herself. "What happened?" she asked.

He fell into a chair, his face contorted with grief. "Grandpa's dead."

"Oh, no. I'm so sorry, Lani." She put her arms around him, trying to comfort him. "He lived a good, long life."

"I miss him already." Lani buried his head in her shoulder and his body shook with sorrow.

"I do, too," thought Sarah. "I do, too."

The next few days brought a constant march of family and friends, bringing food and trying to comfort the old woman. The masses spilled out of the small family house and into the yard. Children played and shouted, unaware of the tragedy. Mrs. Waikaloa sat inconsolable in her overstuffed chair, eating nothing, but rocking and humming to herself.

Lani walked around like a ghost during those few days and Sarah missed seeing his smile. She, on the other hand, had miraculously regained her health. She checked out of the hotel and brought her possessions to Lani's tiny house. During the day, she helped out with the food preparation and clean-up, finding herself accepted and warmly welcomed into his family. At night, as they lay together, she held Lani close to her while he talked endlessly of his grandfather and of all the boyhood memories they had shared.

During the Kahuna's funeral, it seemed that the whole island turned out to say good-bye. He was cherished and well-loved by all who knew him. Sarah sat in the first pew in the local church with Lani, his grandmother, auntie, and sisters, who all sobbed loudly. Sarah was amazed at the seemingly endless grief. She held Lani's hand throughout the short ceremony, wishing she could say or do something to make him feel comforted.

Afterwards, a huge party ensued at the Waikaloa property. The immediate transformation in the grieving family took Sarah by surprise, as everyone, including Moana, laughed and joked and ate.

"What's happened?" she whispered to Lani.

"It's our way," he explained without explaining anything. "We are celebrating grandpa's life."

After all the revelers had left, Lani took Sarah back to his house. He stretched his long, lean body and began to undress. "I'm glad that's over," he commented and yawned. "I'm really tired."

Sarah was at a loss for words, confused at his sudden shift in attitude.

"I'm not uncaring," he seemed to pick up her thoughts. "I still love and miss Grandpa. We believe in not holding back our feelings, but to feel them deeply. Then we release our feelings and go on with our lives."

She looked at him, with one eyebrow cocked, challenging him.

"Well, most of us, most of the time," he assented. He smiled broadly, dimples flaring. "Come here, you delicious morsel."

Sarah flew into his arms. "Mmmm, I've missed you so much," she murmured.

"I've missed you, too." He looked at her as if he was seeing her for the first time in days. "You seem better. How do you feel?"

She checked internally. "I'm feeling…fine."

"No headaches?"

"No, they've gone away."

"Well, well." He seemed very pleased.

"I probably ought to go back to the doctor, though."

"Don't you remember what grandpa said? Not to continue with the treatments."

"I remember. But I'd like to get a second opinion."

"Whatever you think is best," he agreed without argument. He hugged her so close, she squealed.

"Lani, too hard."

"Sorry, sweetie. I could just eat you up." He yawned again. "I need a shower."

"Me, too." She looked at him meaningfully.

"The tub's pretty small. We'll be crowded."

"I don't mind."

He grinned and took her by the hand, leading the way. Then he turned the two creaky handles on the old water fixture, adjusting them until it was the perfect temperature. He stepped into the old porcelain tub and helped her in. He poured a handful of aromatic liquid soap from a container and began soaping her back.

Sarah leaned into him, and closed her eyes, inhaling the delicate almond fragrance from the soap.

He spread the slippery foam over her belly and then massaged it around her breasts in a slow, circular motion. He lingered over her nipples, teasingly running his fingers over them.

"Your hands feel marvelous," she said.

"I'm glad you like it," he murmured in reply. Then he moved his powerful, but gentle hands up around her neck, down over her shoulders and still further down to her thighs. "Your skin is so soft and smooth." He kissed the back of her ears and nibbled on her neck, then turned her around to face him. Putting his arms solidly around her, he pressed his taut masculine body against her soft feminine one. "How's that feel?"

"Wonderful," she replied.

"I love you, Sarah," he whispered breathlessly into her ear.

"I love you, too, Lani."

"Marry me?"

"Yes," was her simple reply.

Lani kissed her, his excitement pressing against her body and they made slow, leisurely love throughout the moonlit night.

Chapter 16

Brothers

The next morning, a radiant Sarah nudged Lani in the ribs. "Wake up, sleepy head."

"What time is it?"

"It's late, I think."

"Mmmm." He rolled over to try to sleep again.

She gently poked him again. "I think I should go see Dr. Namagushi."

He turned quickly back. "Whatever for?"

"I want to make sure I'm all better."

"But grandpa said…"

"But I have to know." She kissed him lightly. "Humor me, sweetheart."

"Okay," and he hugged the sweet woman to his chest.

Sarah made an appointment with her doctor and another series of medical tests were performed at Lani's insistence. When the doctor showed the couple the results, he was incredulous. "The tumor is completely gone. Either the first tests were wrong or…" He didn't finish.

"Maybe it's a spontaneous remission," she offered.

"Could be," he agreed reluctantly. Then he smiled, his white teeth gleaming. "Whatever the reason, I'm very glad for you."

"Thank you," she beamed.

"Why don't you come back in about six months and we'll check to make sure it hasn't returned."

"All right," she replied happily. "But I don't think it will."

"Congratulations," and he held out his hand.

"We're going to be married," she added, shaking his hand.

"Then double congratulations!" and he shook Lani's hand vigorously as well.

After they had driven home from the doctor's, Sarah became very excited. She paced up and down in his small house, then turned to her lover. "We need to go see Jim."

"Is that necessary?" Lani asked, suddenly wary.

"Yes," replied the determined woman. "It is."

"I don't know. After all you've told me, I think we should forget the past," Lani countered.

"I think this is very important," she insisted.

Lani had learned that Sarah was headstrong, but for reasons he had learned to respect. "Okay, but shouldn't we call him first?"

"Yes," then took out her phone and dialed Jim's number. "Jim? This is Sarah. Hi, yourself. I was wondering if I could come over? Um, hm. In about an hour? Okay. See you then."

Lani looked at her quizzically.

"Come on," she pulled on his arm.

"Are you sure you know what you're doing?"

"Yes, my love." She kissed him, coaxing him out of the house.

"You're the boss," and his face dimpled.

She smiled in appreciation.

When they arrived at his house, Jim was waiting outside. He acted surprised to see Lani, however.

Sarah got out of the black SUV, walked over to the pianist and held out her hand. "Hi, Jim."

Jim took her proffered hand and kissed it, without relinquishing it. "Aloha, Sarah. I'm glad you came. I was wondering if I was ever going to see you again."

She squeezed his hand. "Me, too."

Jim frowned seeing Lani coming up behind her.

"You two have already met. Jim Diamond. Lani Waikaloa."

The two tentatively shook hands.

"So, what's up?" Jim asked Sarah awkwardly.

"I want to invite you to our wedding," she said enthusiastically.

Both Lani and Jim were obviously shocked, but for completely different reasons.

"Uh, that's great," Jim responded with a reluctance in his voice that didn't match his words.

Lani whispered in Sarah's ear, "You should've asked me first."

"Shhh," she replied. "I know what I'm doing."

"Come on in. Let's toast to the bride," said Jim politely and led them into his house. He poured them each a glass of vodka and they clinked glasses. "To your happiness, Sarah. Yours, too," he said to Lani. His sorrowful face tore at Sarah's heart.

"And your happiness, too, Jim," she added.

"That's impossible now," he answered morosely.

"It's time to let go of something you can't have, maybe never could."

"Perhaps." He shrugged.

"Trust me. You can't."

Jim's shoulders sagged.

Then Sarah took a deep breath. "Jim, I have something else to ask you."

"I'd do anything for you." He looked at her expectantly.

"I know," she smiled. "And I'm grateful for that."

He shrugged.

She took hold of both his hands and looked deeply into his eyes. "I'd like you to forgive me."

"Isn't it me who should be asking for forgiveness?" he asked bleakly.

"Well?" she continued without answering his question.

"Okay. I forgive you, Sarah."

"Thank you, Jim," and she sighed in relief.

He studied her luminous face. "Maybe I've missed something, but you act like you know something I don't know."

Lani spoke up. "Sarah's cancer is gone."

The blonde man looked suddenly ecstatic. "That's terrific!" Then he mentally counted off the days since he had last seen her. "But how…" He wrinkled up his face in confusion and doubt.

"It's a miracle," Lani continued.

"Yes, and you're part of it," she motioned to Jim.

"But I haven't done anything. I haven't even seen you in…"

"We've been having dreams about you," Lani interrupted.

Sarah looked at her fiancé with a new appreciation.

"No kidding? I've had some doozies myself lately," replied Jim.

"Tell me about them," Sarah encouraged.

"Well, I dream I'm a warrior kind of guy, disfigured you know? Maybe from some battle or something. I have this big shark's tooth necklace I'm wearing." Jim stopped.

"Uh, huh." She looked knowingly at Lani who was listening attentively.

"And I see myself in a little shack and there's a baby crying and I can't comfort it. I always feel crummy when I wake up."

"Sarah? Are you thinking what I'm thinking?" Lani exclaimed.

"I'm right there with you," she answered.

"Jim and I…Grandfather's story…the dreams…"

"That's right."

"We were brothers!"

Jim interjected. "What are you talking about?"

"I would really like for you to come to our wedding!" Lani said impulsively, dimpling deeply.

Sarah thought she could see gold light shining from his heart.

"You're both nuts!" Jim commented, but he melted in the glow. "Yeah, sure. I'd love to." His face and body looked more relaxed.

"Oh, good," replied Sarah.

"Why don't I arrange for the reception to be held at the resort? I'm sure I can get you a good price. And I know a great pianist…"

They both hugged him in response.

"Hey, be careful of the shirt," Jim said kiddingly. "I just ironed it."

Epilogue

Mahina as Sarah

My beloved and I were married in that little chapel in Kileaua. Lani's enormous contingent of friends and family were packed together in ecstatic and noisy celebration. I could smell the plumeria as it wafted its sweet perfume through the open windows of the church as one of Lani's cousins walked me down the aisle. Dr. Namagushi was in attendance as was my mother and my former editor Sam Johnston, who had both flown in for the occasion. I wore a white orchid lei over my wedding dress, which set off my long red hair to perfection.

"You look beautiful," Lani murmured to me when we met at the altar. "I wish grandpa was here," he whispered.

"Maybe he's watching us from above," I spoke quietly to the handsome man at my side. Silently I blessed the old Kahuna. Then I handed my bouquet to Malia, one of Lani's many cousins, who stood with me as maid of honor, as Lani and I recited our vows. The minister proclaimed us man and wife.

Jim, as promised, had arranged our reception at the Kapaa resort as a wedding present, but many of the women brought homemade dishes anyway. Auntie, of course, brought her famous two-finger poi. The Alapai family musicians played in a way that touched me deeply. When they sang "The Hawaiian Wedding" song in their native language, Lani hugged me close to him. I could feel his heart pounding rapidly.

I noticed that Jim danced often with Malia, a classic Polynesian beauty who was studying music at the University of Hawaii. He consented to play the piano for us as well, while she in turn never took her glistening dark eyes off him. Later they left together in Jim's silver Mercedes. Jim and Malia were married before the year was over.

A few months after our wedding, we found out I was pregnant. Lani said, "If it's a boy, let's name him Mamu. Have him learn the ancient Kahuna ways."

I wholeheartedly agreed. The growing child inside me jumped with joy.

www.ingramcontent.com/pod-product-compliance
Lightning Source LLC
Chambersburg PA
CBHW061209170626
46809CB00003B/1302